THE MASS AND MARY BROWN

For
John and Paddy Treasure
and Fr Pat Kelly SMA,
John and Marg Blatchford
and Fr Peter Keeling,
good companions on the way

ANTHEA DOVE

The Mass and Mary Brown

THE COLUMBA PRESS
DUBLIN 2001

THE COLUMBA PRESS
55A Spruce Avenue, Stillorgan Industrial Park,
Blackrock, Co Dublin

First edition 2001
Designed by Bill Bolger
Origination by
The Columba Press
Printed in Ireland by
Colour Books Ltd, Dublin

ISBN 1 85607 329 7

Acknowledgements
The author and publisher gratefully acknowledge the permission of the following to use material in their copyright: Excerpts from the English translation of *The Roman Missal* © 1973, International Committee on English in the Liturgy, Inc. All rights reserved. Biblical quotations are from *The Jerusalem Bible,* published and copyright 1966, 1967, 1968, by Darton, Longman and Todd Ltd and Doubleday & Co Inc and used by permission of the publishers. The quotation from Psalm 62 is copyright © 1963, The Grail (England). 'This is my body' is copyright © 1978 Bud John Songs/EMI Christian Music Publishing, administered by CopyCare, PO Box 77, Hailsham, BN27 3EF, UK, and used by permission. 'In bread we bring you, Lord' is copyright © Kevin Mayhew Ltd. Used by permission from *Hymns Old and New,* licence no. 001192. The prayer from *The Alternative Service Book 1980* is copyright © The Archbishops' Council and is reproduced by permission.

Copyright © 2001, Anthea Dove

CONTENTS

Preface	7
Mary Brown	9
Introduction	11
The Mass and Mary Brown	13
Mary Brown at a Baptism	45
Mary Brown goes to Confession	54
Mary Brown and the Eucharist	62
Mary Brown and Confirmation	68
Mary Brown and Marriage	75
Mary Brown and Ordination	84
Mary Brown and the Sacrament of Anointing	91
Mary Brown goes on Retreat	102

Preface

Mary Brown is not me, but we are alike in many respects. Like Mary, I am growing old, I have several children and grandchildren. Like her, I love the church, like her I struggle sometimes with my faith. And like her I am full of questions and full of thankfulness.

This book describes the thoughts and feelings of Mary as she goes to Mass on a Sunday, receives or attends the various sacraments, and goes on retreat. I have written it for two sorts of people. First, for those, very many I believe, who share in Mary's weaknesses and strengths. These are people whose religious devotion, in spite of their best intentions, often takes second place to their concerns for the overriding events and difficulties in their lives. They are the faithful, but they are not always the understood. Over the years I have listened to many lay people talking of their problems with the church and saying how hard it is to relate what is happening in their day-to-day lives with what happens when they go to Mass.

The second kind of people I have in mind in writing about Mary fall into a different category. I have read a number of spiritual books on the Mass and the sacraments, written by priests and theologians, and I have listened to countless sermons on the subject. Many of them have been instructive and helpful, but I have come to believe that very few priests have a true idea of how it feels to be a 'person in the pew', a lay person on the receiving end. So this book is for them too.

Mary Brown

My name is Mary Brown and I am a Roman Catholic. I was born into a Catholic family, educated at two Catholic schools and married a Catholic man. I go to Mass on Sundays and sometimes in the week. I take my turn at cleaning the church and helping with the parish bazaar in winter and the fete in summer. When I stand up on a Sunday morning to say the Creed, I believe every word of it.

Now I am getting old. I am a grandmother. And the other day an old friend of mine in the parish, Tony, who was an altar server for as long as I can remember and is now a eucharistic minister, said to me,

'You know, Mary, as Roman Catholics we are on the last bus.' Then he shrugged and added, 'No we're not, we're running after the last bus!'

He laughed ruefully but I hadn't the heart to laugh with him. The last bus, a sinking ship – these images grieve me. I feel confused and discouraged and yet keep on, as others keep on. I suppose we are still what used to be called 'the faithful'.

For me it's very hard. My family is my life. My faith is my life. When the children were small, all of us, together with their father, would pray together each evening. But now I don't even talk to them about God any more, because they either laugh at me or become defensive because they think I'm disappointed in them.

I go on loving them, of course, whatever they say, whatever they do. And at the same time I go on attending church and being a 'good' Catholic. My children are good too, even the ones who are no longer Christians, who no longer believe in God.

My children's values and attitudes and ideas are those of the world, of the society in which we live. Sometimes these coincide with the values of the gospel, sometimes they are in opposition to the teachings of scripture and the church.

If anyone were to ask me to choose between my family and my faith I would be completely unable to do so. I live all the time now in this tension, between the centre of my life that is my family and the centre of my life that is God.

And yet, somehow, just sometimes, I feel there is no contradiction after all. For perhaps it's true that where there is love, there is God.

Introduction

> One of the crowd went up,
> And knelt before the Paten and the Cup,
> Received the Lord, returned in peace, and prayed
> Close to my side. Then in my heart I said:
>
> O Christ, in this man's life -
> This stranger who is Thine - in all his strife,
> All his felicity, his good and ill,
> In the assaulted stronghold of his will,
>
> I do confess Thee here
> Alive within this life …..
>
> Alice Meynell, *The Unknown God*

When I read this poem, I thought of Mary Brown. For all the wanderings of her mind and all the fluctuations of her emotions during the Mass, Mary has a profound sense of awe and humility when she goes to receive Holy Communion. And this awareness of the wonder and greatness of God in no way conflicts with her sensitivity to her fellow worshippers.

For Mary, the Mass is about her relationship to God, and, bound up with that, it is about her relationship with those whose lives touch hers, the persons sitting 'close to her side', her community, the people of God.

The Mass and Mary Brown

It's just like me – I deliberately set off early for Mass and arrive late.

It's such a beautiful morning. After days of continuous rain the sky is blue and cloudless, the sun feels warm on my face and suddenly the big lime tree in the park is coming into leaf. I feel like dancing and singing but of course I don't. I'm much too old and sadly too respectable. But I just have to stop and take a long look at that tree. Somehow, the older I get, the more I appreciate the loveliness of spring and the more I want to praise God for the wonder of creation. So I dawdle a while, lifting my heart to him in thanksgiving.

Then I begin to walk quickly because, although I have plenty of time, I do like a few moments' quiet before Mass, just to settle and compose myself, I suppose. But today it is not to be.

I meet Henry Dawson shuffling along with his stick. His face brightens when he sees me – I don't think he knows many people. I can see he wants to talk and I know it will be about Elsie. He tells me she has full-blown Alzheimer's now and he can only get out for half an hour each day while the home help is with her. It's really touching, the way Henry talks about Elsie. Obviously he still dotes on her even now when she doesn't know who he is, and she makes so much work. He looks worn out, poor old man, and I haven't the heart to cut him short – he so much wants to talk. But of course, when I finally get away, I realise I'll be late. It's ten o'clock already.

I can't run any more because of my arthritis, but I walk as fast as I can and they are still singing the entrance hymn when I arrive breathless in the porch. It's one of my favourites: 'We have come into his house.' It's easy to sing and the words exactly express what is happening: 'We have come into his house and gathered in his name, to worship him.' In some ways I still prefer the old hymns with their beautiful words, like 'All people that on earth do dwell' and 'Praise my soul the King of Heaven', but there's something about this one, although it's so simple, that makes me glad to be a part of our church community, faithfully gathered here every Sunday to worship God.

Doris gives me a big smile. She's the ideal person to welcome people and you get a smile and, if you're lucky, a hug too. It's the same if you're late, the same if you're a stranger.

The church is pretty full and I have to go nearly

to the front before I can find a seat. Then I see it's Father Joe and I am glad. We never know whether it will be him or Father Crane, who is actually our parish priest and has been here for at least twenty years. I guess most people hope it will be the young priest saying Mass, except for the old sticklers (and the not-so-old sticklers!) who can't stand change of any sort and won't hear a word of criticism of any priest. Well, I do try not to criticise or judge anybody, honestly I do, but sometimes I get exasperated and say out loud what perhaps I should keep to myself.

Father Crane is not actually very old, in fact he's a lot younger than me, but the sad truth is, he's no good with people. He doesn't visit the housebound and he won't listen. It's easy to see he doesn't like women, but I suspect he doesn't much like any layfolk. I suppose I should try to understand the poor chap. He certainly doesn't look happy, and I guess he's lonely.

Young Father Joe, now, is very easy to like. He's friendly and open and you can tell he really cares about the parishioners, especially the poor and the people in trouble. He's great with young people too, a lot more of them have started to come to Mass now he's here.

Well, the hymn's over now. I managed to sing the last verse though it was hard to keep the tune standing next to Norman Chalmers who is tone deaf but insists on singing at the top of his voice.

As we begin the penitential bit I say a quick prayer, asking God to help me to concentrate on what's happening in the Mass because I get so hopelessly distracted. I so seldom go to confession nowadays, so it seems important to have a good think about my sins at least once a week. Now that I'm an old woman, it's like when I was a child, always the same old sins, boring trivial sins that none the less show a lack of love for God, and it isn't long before I'm distracted again. That's not surprising, really, as Jenny is so much in my thoughts today …

* * *

My feelings are so muddled. Most of all, I suppose, I ache for Jenny. I long to be there with her, to comfort her, afterwards. But when I offered to go, she said No.

And I feel so guilty, not so much because abortion is a sin and a terrible sin at that, but because I did nothing to try to persuade Jen to change her mind. I simply listened and told her I would be thinking of her.

But as soon as I put the phone down I began to feel ashamed. After all I am a Catholic, I am Jenny's mother and although she walked away from the church years ago, she was certainly brought up to believe that abortion was wrong. Yet something – perhaps the recognition that Jenny is an adult and must be free to make her own decisions – prevented me from ringing her back. Instead I went to the florist's and ordered some daffodils to be sent for her tomorrow, when it's all over. Yellow is her favourite colour …

'Lord, have mercy' Father Joe is saying.

'Lord, have mercy' I respond fervently, and silently, I pray, 'on me, on Jenny, on all poor sinners.'

* * *

We're singing the Gloria. I like that. Every time I say or sing these words I think how little time I give to praising and thanking God. And yet my life is just full of blessings, my cup runneth over as it says in the psalm. Sometimes I wonder if I should join a charismatic group. They are always praising God. But no, I know Vin would put his foot down. He's always telling me I do too much and he's probably right, poor Vin.

The two little girls in the bench in front of me,

Katie and Lucy Hartley, are singing away, quite unselfconscious. They look delightful with their shining hair and matching pink frocks and white socks, and I remember, with something of a pang, how it was when mine were young. There were seven of them to get ready. I'd wash their hair the night before and Vincent would clean all our shoes. I put all their clothes out, everything clean for Sunday, but even so it was always such a scramble to get them all ready in time for Mass.

We were very strict in those days, Vin and I. We didn't allow any whispering or giggling or even let them turn round. But as far as I can remember, our two little daughters, Jenny and Anne, were angelic, just like these two in front of me. As for the boys, well that's another story. We couldn't take our eyes off them for a second without at least one of them getting up to some mischief.

I close my eyes and listen to the words of the Opening Prayer.

'Heavenly Father and God of mercy,
we no longer look for Jesus among the dead,
for he is alive and has become the Lord of life.
From the waters of death you raise us with him
and renew your gift of life within us.

Increase in our minds and hearts

the risen life we share with Christ
and help us to grow as your people
towards the fullness of eternal life with you.'

The words are beautiful. I specially like 'help us to grow as your people'. It's a miracle how we can still go on growing and changing and learning, however old and tired and busy and feeble we are …

We're sitting down now. That's good – for some reason I feel quite tired today. I hear the tap of heels on the hard floor of the aisle and I catch a whiff of expensive scent. I know, without looking, who is going to do the first reading.

* * *

Sure enough, it's Shirley Hunter, making her way gracefully to the lectern, putting on her gold-rimmed specs, smiling graciously at the congregation and beginning to read from the Acts of the Apostles.

I know I have no right to criticise, I know I must not be judgmental, but the plain truth is, I don't like Shirley. I never have. It's sad that we've known each other since we started at the infant school, but we couldn't get on, right from the beginning. I know I've got to try, I've got to work on it, I mustn't give up. But she's such a snob, and so sure of herself, and nothing seems to go wrong in her life …

To be fair, I have to admit Shirley does read beautifully, better than any of us. But I smile inwardly when I realise what the reading is. It's all about the first Christians and how they lived in harmony, sharing everything. Shirley reads with such feeling but I can't imagine her giving as much as a lift in her car to someone unless she knew them well and approved of them. Oh dear, there I go again, making unkind judgements.

* * *

'Give thanks to the Lord, for he is good,
for his love has no end,' we respond to the psalm.

How far I am from being like God! My love certainly has its limits. But I love this psalm, especially the line, 'The Lord is my strength and my song.'

For me, to say that God is my song means that he is that spring of joy inside me which (sometimes at least) I am aware of, even though at the same time I am weighed down by so many sorrows and anxieties. There's something sustaining about this, about the Lord, my strength and my song, even now when I am worried sick about Jenny and her abortion, Vincent and his depression and little Toby, our grandson, who has a huge birthmark on his face. And then there's Johnny, our youngest. I'm pretty sure he's on drugs …

Shirley's heels are clicking again. Surely that's a patronising smile she gives young Dave Williams as they pass on the sanctuary steps? I'm nervous for Dave. I don't think he's ever read in church before and I remember he's got a slight stammer. I wonder who persuaded him to read, then I glance across at Father Joe and sense that he feels much as I do. He's silently willing Dave to cope. Of course, I remember now, Dave is in Joe's Youth Group.

Unfortunately it is not an easy reading. It's from one of St Peter's letters, with long unwieldy sentences. But I begin to relax. Dave is doing fine. His voice is pleasant, his local accent contrasts with Shirley's smooth educated tones and is good to listen to. I begin to notice the words and think about their meaning. They seem like an answer to what I was thinking about the psalm.

'Through your faith, God's power will guard you until the salvation which has been prepared for you is revealed at the end of time. This is a cause of great joy to you, even though you may for a short time have to bear being plagued with all sorts of trials; so that, when Jesus Christ is revealed, your faith will have been tested and proved like gold – only it is more precious than gold, which is corruptible even though it bears testing by fire — and then you will have praise and glory and honour.'

I don't want praise and glory and honour; I just want to hold on to my faith.

Towards the end, Dave seems more confident. He slows down a bit, and looks up from the lectionary at the congregation. He leads us in the gospel acclamation, and then steps down from the lectern, no longer self-conscious but holding his head up. You can almost hear him think, 'Phew! Thank God that's over!'

* * *

There's something the matter with Father Joe. He looks very pale but I don't think he's ill. Perhaps he's unhappy? Whatever is wrong, it's made him very tense.

I've heard a rumour that he's gay, and Phyllis Harris, who goes to Mass every day without fail and has the cruellest tongue in the parish, said he ought not to be allowed to be in charge of the Youth Club, in case he abused some of the young boys. I lost my temper then and told Phyllis she was ignorant and prejudiced. She hasn't spoken to me since.

As it happens I am certain that Father Joe is not homosexual. I could tell that from the way he related to Jenny and Anne when he came round to see us and they both happened to be at home. I remember that after he left I found Anne looking quite wistful. 'What a pity he's a priest,' she said, 'He's really cool.'

For myself, it makes no difference whether he's gay or not. I just find him a nice fellow, friendly, compassionate and hard-working. And I happen to know he's a man of prayer. I feel concerned that today something is obviously disturbing him.

Father Joe reads the gospel well. I only half listen because I'm thinking about Vin, but it hardly matters because after all these years I know the story of Doubting Thomas inside out. I love all the resurrection stories. I never get tired of hearing them, and trying to imagine what it must have been like to be there, to be Mary Magdalene or Thomas or the two disciples on the road to Emmaus.

Thomas has my sympathy. Who would blame him for not believing? And the moment when his eyes are opened and he does believe and he cries, 'My Lord and my God!' – at that moment I always want to cry.

I'm surprised, like everyone else, when Father Joe tells us that the Youth Club members are going to enact the story for us. I wonder if Father Crane knows about this. We don't usually have drama in our church.

I expect the young people to be awkward and to giggle and forget their lines, so I'm pretty amazed and impressed when they put on a simple, serious and very moving performance.

I know the boy, Shane, who takes the part of Thomas. He lives down our street and he's a bit of a hooligan. He's the eldest of four children of Lisa Pigott, a single mother who's never married. She is a Catholic and all the children have been to St Theresa's, our Primary School – the youngest, little Jade, is still there. I know Lisa works at the supermarket on Sundays, so she won't be here, watching Shane, which is sad.

Father Joe says we'll now have a few minutes' silence to reflect on the gospel. When Father Crane says we'll have a time of silence, he breaks it himself thirty seconds later, but Father Joe takes this sort of thing seriously. I'm glad; I would like to reflect on the gospel and I pray that God will keep my mind focused on it, for once, this morning.

I have heard people, wise people, say that doubt can be a good thing, a healthy thing. But for me, it's frightening. If I were to lose my faith, it would be like falling from the safety of a ship into a bottomless ocean, unable to swim.

My worst doubts came when I was sixteen, and

my best friend died of cancer. I made a solemn vow then to renounce my belief in God, and I actually said, aloud, 'I'm sorry, God, I can't believe in you any more,' without realising the irony of such a statement. By the time I was seventeen, my faith was restored, but from time to time it has wavered again, especially in the face of human suffering. Yet always, and for this I thank God with all my heart, the sure and certain hope that is faith is re-kindled. It feels as though God will never let me go.

Thomas is one of those bible characters with whom it is easy to identify: stubborn, foolish, humiliated, and then suddenly caught up in an exchange of tremendous love, the love of his Lord for him and his own in response.

Norman, next to me, has gone to sleep. He's not exactly snoring, but I can hear the steady rumble of his breathing. Susan, the mother of Katie and Lucy in front of me, is not meditating on the gospel either. She is concentrating on keeping the children quiet. But they are behaving perfectly well, both looking at their picture books about Jesus. It seems a pity that Susan can't relax.

I look at Father Joe. He is sitting quite still, his hands open on his lap, the very picture of someone rapt in meditation, and yet I still sense that there is something troubling him. Perhaps it's my overactive imagination playing tricks. It's nothing to do with me anyway and I doubt if I'll ever find out what's wrong. That's if anything is.

* * *

Now Father Joe is coming forward. Fr Crane still uses the pulpit but Joe prefers to speak from the altar steps. He has a quiet voice but he's wearing one of those hidden microphone things so we can hear him easily.

I thought perhaps with the drama and then the silence we would get away without a sermon to day, but no such luck. I know this is the wrong attitude especially as Joe is a very good preacher, but I'm longing to get back to Vin to see how he is this morning.

It's as though the young priest has read my thoughts. He smiles at us and says 'I won't be keeping you for long. Perhaps after the drama we all have enough to think about, but I just wanted to say a few words.'

I listen. I always listen to the sermon, whoever is preaching. I know I should pay proper attention right through the Mass, and I do try to, I pray to God to help me to concentrate, but I seem to have so many things on my mind. And although I know it's no excuse, I've heard the words of the Mass a million, well, very many times before and I suppose that's why they wash over me. Whereas the sermon is always different, and I always hope to learn something. It's almost like getting nourished when you're hungry. This sermon is not about what I thought it would be. It's not about doubt, but fear.

Fr Joe read out his text, twice: 'the doors were closed in the room where the disciples were, for fear of the Jews'. He always speaks without notes, unlike Fr Crane who reads his sermons, and he preaches as though he is talking to each one of us personally, at any rate that's how it feels to me.

And as usual, he's hit the nail on the head. He says he thinks most of us are ruled by fear. Well, I know I am. When I wake up every morning I am afraid, afraid to find out how Vin is, afraid my arthritis will be worse, afraid of the telephone bill being too high, afraid of discovering what Johnny's up to … the list seems endless.

Joe reminds us of how many times Jesus said, 'Do not be afraid.' He says that Jesus understands our fearfulness. We should place our trust in Jesus, but not the trust that all our prayers will be answered the way we want them to be; we should put our absolute trust in God's unwavering love for each one of us.

He's finished! It really was a short homily and it's left me feeling comforted and a little stronger.

It seems to me that a good sermon is one that reaches us where we are, that impinges on the reality of our lives. And it will only be effective, I think, if the preacher somehow identifies with us who are listening, if it comes across that he too is struggling on his spiritual journey. But perhaps I ask too much; after all I couldn't preach a sermon to save my life!

* * *

It's time for the Creed now, my very worst time for distraction. I wish we didn't have it so often, then I'd be more likely to think about the words that stream so automatically from my mouth. Surely it would have more effect if we only said it at, say, Christmas and Easter and Pentecost, or on holidays of obligation?

I wonder if Vincent is still in bed. The depression makes it so hard for him to face the day, but once he's up and dressed at least he goes through the motions of being alive. Poor Vin! If only there was something I could do to help! I try being attentive and sympathetic; it doesn't work. I try being cheerful; that doesn't work either. It's as though he's undergone a complete personality change, Vin who was always laughing and joking, such fun to be with. I would never have imagined that being made redundant would do this to him.

I wonder if he'll get to Mass today. We always used to come together. And Vin was such a stickler for the rules – I've known him to go to Mass with a high temperature when there was a blizzard blowing! Father Joe says that in his condition it's not important if he misses Mass, and I agree, only it might take him out of himself for a while?

I wish I could talk to Vincent about Johnny. I'm sure he's taking something and I don't know what to do about it. But I can hardly burden Vin when he's in this state ... Oh, Lord, the Creed is over. I said all the words and didn't think about one of them.

We wait to see who will be saying the Bidding Prayers today. Father Crane lets anyone who wishes to make up the prayers and read them. He does vet them first, of course, but I think it's surprisingly liberal of him to allow it, and it does mean we pay attention!

Oh good. It's Grace Trelawney. If there's a saint in our parish I reckon it's Grace. She's a lovely woman, a West Indian married to a Cornishman. She has a beautiful serene face and her name suits her perfectly.

I know what the prayers will mostly be about – justice and peace issues. Grace is the chairperson of the parish justice and peace group and she is very concerned about global warming. She has asked me more than once to join, but I haven't committed myself yet.

However, the first prayer isn't about justice.

'Lord, open our eyes to see clearly, so that we may truly understand our sisters and brothers. Help us to stand in their shoes, so that we may be slow to judge and quick to love. Lord, hear us.'

For a second or two I stare at Grace, thinking, 'That prayer is for me. How could she have known?'

Then I close my eyes and I begin to pray fervently. I pray for Shirley Hunter and for Phyllis Harris, the only two people I dislike. I think about them both, and realise how little I know about their lives, about what makes them tick, about their relationships, their sorrows. I pray that I will get to know them better, to understand them, perhaps to love them. I thank God for Grace and open my eyes to see that she is already on her way back to her place. I haven't heard any of the other prayers! I'm dismayed until I remember I can easily get a copy of them later.

* * *

It's time for the Offertory. It's good to be sitting down again. I take a pound from my purse. I can't afford any more since Vin lost his job. When old Richard Barlow passes the plate along our row, I slip in my pound coin, hoping no one will notice.

I am watching the children serving on the sanctuary. The smallest is Anthony Walsh, my friend Clare's son. He looks like a cherub, and he's a little imp. He's giggling now and whispering to Sanjay whose family comes from South India. Sanjay is obviously trying to behave well, probably conscious of his father's eye on him from the front bench. I don't know the name of the girl server, but she is taking it all very seriously.

When Father Joe moves towards the steps, ready to receive the offerings, the little girl follows and stands next to him. Young Anthony seizes his chance. He creeps up behind her and tugs at her long blond hair. Poor child! Her face goes red and I can see her squeeze her eyes in an effort to hold back tears, but she stays where she is, standing up straight. I glance across at Clare. From the look on her face I guess that Anthony will be in big trouble after Mass.

The organ starts up and I recognise 'In bread we bring you, Lord' – my favourite offertory hymn. Deliberately, I pay attention to the words, particularly at the end:

'Take all that daily toil
plants in our hearts' poor soil,
take all we start and spoil,
each hopeful dream,
the chances we have missed,
the graces we resist,
Lord, in thy Eucharist, take and redeem.'

It seems to me that whoever wrote this hymn knows all about life. What are my hopeful dreams? They are, of course, dreams for my family. Perhaps I should have hopeful dreams for the world, too, for the end of global warming, for the hungry in developing countries, for the poor in our own country, for peace … the problems are all so vast. Maybe if I did join the justice and peace group I'd learn more and I'd be with like-minded people …

The offertory procession is coming up the aisle now. Today it's the O'Driscoll family, father, mother, daughter and son. The son, Peter, has mild cerebral palsy, and I think how brave it is of them to let him carry the wafers. I suppose most people are like me, holding their breath.

At the very last minute Peter lurches into his sister. She holds tight to the jug of wine, but some of the wafers tip out of Peter's basket and scatter on the floor. Behind me I hear a mutter of disapproval, and am about to turn round and confront somebody when I remember my prayer about tolerance.

Naughty Anthony is the first to start picking up the hosts. He carefully blows on each one – presumably to get rid of any dust – before he puts them back in the basket which Peter is still holding. Some of us can't help laughing, and this includes Father Joe, but he composes himself in time to thank Peter for his offering. This will be something to tell Vincent. It might even make him laugh.

It's humbling to think that I am myself part of what is being offered to God. I suppose I am no more a sinner than the rest of the congregation, but certainly I feel unworthy and pretty useless. What can God do with someone like me? I have so many needs, so many burdens.

And then I remember that God can use even the most unlikely material to bring his love and peace and joy to others, and I whisper a quick prayer: 'All that I am I give to you.'

* * *

Now Fr Joe is praying over the gifts:
'Lord, through faith and baptism
We have become a new creation.'

I have to say I don't feel like a new creation. I feel old and tired, and if I'm truthful, I sometimes feel a bit sorry for myself. God knows I try, I try all the time to be a good wife and mother, let alone a good Christian. Everyone – Vin, my family, the neighbours in our street and I expect most of the people who know me in this parish – think I'm strong and reliable and the sort of person they can share their troubles with. That's nice, of course, in a way, but it seems that nobody knows how much I long, just for once, for somebody to take care of *me,* to listen to *my* problems, to settle me in a comfy chair by the fire and bring me a cup of tea ... Oh, but that's despicable! What am I thinking of? Here I am sitting in Mass, not paying attention, wallowing in self-pity when I've got so much more than most folk, when I don't know what it's like really to suffer: to be tortured, in prison, a refugee, an asylum seeker, incurably sick ... I'm brought up short out of this reverie by a chuckle. I see the little ones in front of me, Katie and Lucy, tickling each other and giggling. Their mother gives each of them a sharp slap that makes me wince and then I realise it's time to stand for the Preface.

Ashamed of myself, I listen carefully to the beginning:

'Father, all-powerful and ever-living God,
we do well always and everywhere to give you thanks.'

How true that is! I begin to go through all the things I have to be thankful for: blessings without number.

I think of each of my children and grandchildren and realise that although I have serious worries about some of them I also have very much to be grateful for, and for some reason think of Charlie, my youngest grandson, a healthy happy bright-faced child who as far as I know has never been inside a church. I did so hope James and Fiona would have him baptised, but they both think it's better to wait until he's old enough to make up his own mind. I remember how we used to be told that unbaptised babies would end up in Limbo. What a terrible teaching that was! I know very well that God loves Charlie, baptised or not, even more than I do …

Oh dear, the Preface is over and I failed again to listen.

* * *

It's time for the Canon of the Mass. Kneeling is a problem for me. It hurts so much as my knees touch the wooden kneeler and it's hard not to wince. Last week my doctor said I'm unlikely to get a replacement before Christmas, (and that's only for one knee) so I'll have to put up with it. I suppose I should sit and I suppose I don't because I'm too proud. I don't want people to think I'm some sort of invalid.

Oh, good. As soon as Fr Joe says the word 'fountain' I know it's going to be the shortest Canon. I sigh with relief. Not long now. Mass will soon be over and I can get home to Vin. But what sort of attitude is this? It can't be right to want to rush through Mass, can it?

Very firmly, I will myself to concentrate. I think of the Last Supper and Jesus with his friends and when Fr Joe lifts up the host I bow my head because I believe that Jesus is really present at this moment, in this place. I am filled with wonder and reverence which stays with me when the chalice is raised too, and suddenly from nowhere the phrase comes into my head: 'I will draw all people to myself' and I believe that not only I but all of us sinners will one day be embraced in the love of God and held there for all eternity.

Sharply, I bring myself back to the present moment. Fr Joe is saying:

'Remember Leslie whom you have called from this life.

In baptism he died with Christ:

may he also share in his resurrection.'

Leslie Summers was a very old man who died last week. He was a friend of my father's. But my father was an agnostic. He was as kind and unselfish a man as you could meet but he would never have anything to do with the church. Surely, surely, he too would share in Christ's resurrection? Wouldn't he? As often, I feel sad thinking about this. If only my mother could have persuaded him, if only I, his daughter, could have somehow managed it .... And then I remember, again, those comforting words: 'I will draw all people to myself'.

Everyone around me is saying Amen, a good hearty response, and we all get to our feet ready to say the Our Father.

* * *

We are going to sing the prayer today and I'm glad. It's a slow tune and it gives me time to think about the words. 'Give us this day our daily bread' I sing, and I ask myself 'What does this mean?' Can it mean, 'Give me enough food?' I always have enough food. I don't know what it's like to be hungry. But should I not be praying for the African children who are dying at this moment for lack of food? Or maybe, praying is not enough? Maybe I should be doing something? Maybe I could go out there ...of course I couldn't ... sometimes I can be unbelievably silly ...

'Deliver us from evil …' There is so much evil I should like to be delivered from – sin, of course, that goes without saying, but also fear and anxiety and, yes, pain. And as in this prayer I'm praying for all my brothers and sisters, I pray for them to be delivered from hunger and poverty and violence and war and despair.

But Fr Joe is saying: 'Let us offer one another a sign of peace.' At least I can try to do this well. I look into Norman Chalmers' eyes with a smile and shake his hand firmly. Then I lean down to shake the small hands of Katie and Lucy in front of me and their mother gives me a bright smile. I turn round and see Becky Ritson and Verity Smailes standing behind me. Becky shakes my hand warmly but Verity only manages a stiff unsmiling nod. Then from nowhere a scruffy child advances towards Verity. Her nose is running but she's beaming all over her face and she tries to seize Verity's hand in her own sticky one. I catch Becky's eye and stifle a giggle.

Looking round, across the other side of the church, I notice Frances Heyroyd. I'm surprised to see her here because I know she's a Methodist. I wonder if she will go up for communion and hope Fr Joe will not refuse her if she does. Does he know she's not a Catholic? Perhaps he will give her a blessing instead. Can that be right? Somehow I can't imagine Jesus turning anyone away. She is such a devout and good woman, a far better Christian than most of the Catholics I know, myself included.

It's already time for the prayer I never fail to say, and to mean, whatever else I neglect.

'Lord, I am not worthy to receive you,
but only say the word and I shall be healed.'

I have an overwhelming sense of unworthiness as I prepare to receive my God, my King, the Lord of the Universe, into my soul. And yet he is also my friend and brother.

* * *

I decide that although I'm sitting near the front I won't go up for communion immediately so that I can prepare myself better. I'm aware that I have been distracted for so much of the Mass and I want to do this one thing wholeheartedly and well.

Perhaps I would have done better to have closed my eyes because instead of concentrating on prayer I am watching the line of people slowly approach the priest. I see a girl of about sixteen with a low-cut top, bare midriff and green spiky hair. I tell myself sternly not to be judgmental. I see a boy with his hands in his pockets actually chewing gum as he nears the sanctuary. I am shocked by the gum. I see another boy with Downs Syndrome, grinning widely. I see a very old man tottering forward, his head sunk on his chest. And I see Verity Smailes, the very essence of primness and propriety, walking with bowed head and neatly folded hands and all at once I am filled with a huge overwhelming love – a smidgen I guess of what God himself must feel – for all these assorted oddments of his people.

I slip into a place behind a young woman. I recognise her, it's Jessie Holloway, a beautiful dark-haired student who has recently come to the parish. I look ahead. There are six or seven people ahead of Jessie and I can see Fr Joe as he gives each person the host. He looks into their eyes and smiles and says their name if he knows it. I like that. I think of the phrase from Isaiah, 'I have called you by your name.'

Already Jessie is holding out her hands. But to my surprise Fr Joe doesn't smile, doesn't even look at her or use her name. His face flushes dark red. In the space of a second I think I understand everything – he is in love with Jessie – she is in love with him – they are in love … and so I hardly notice when Fr Joe looks into my eyes and smiles and says, 'The

Body of Christ, Mary' and in my heart I fail to respond to Christ's gift of himself to me.

To get back to my place I have to go round by the back of the church and, in a side pew, I notice a woman sitting very still. I am shocked to see tears running down her face and then I realise that it's Agnes Dewar and I know very well why she is crying.

Agnes's husband left her ten years ago. She brought up their four children on her own and then three years ago she met Billy Dewar. They fell in love and after a year were married in the United Reformed Church. Both of them work as volunteers helping people with learning difficulties and Agnes also works tirelessly for the church, cleaning the brass, baking for parish functions and washing up afterwards. But because she is divorced and has remarried, she is not allowed to receive holy communion.

I put my arm round her and murmur foolish things like 'Don't cry' and 'I'm sure it will sort itself out', then I leave her and go back to my place. We are singing 'This is my body, broken for you', and suddenly those words hit home, they penetrate my muddled head and heart and I am able to make a sincere prayer of thankfulness and commitment.

I take from my coat pocket the crumpled piece of paper I always carry with me. Dorothy, one of my Anglican friends, gave it to me. It's a prayer they say after Communion and I find it helpful to say it:

Father of all, we give you thanks and praise,
that when we were still far off you met us
in your Son and brought us home.
Dying and living,
he declared your love, gave us grace,
and opened the gates of glory.
May we who share Christ's body
live his risen life;
we who drink his cup bring life to others;
we whom the Spirit lights give life to the world.
Keep us firm in the hope you have set before us,
so we and all our children shall be free,
and the whole earth live to praise your name;
through Christ our Lord. Amen.

I suppose this is what the Mass is all about – what happens afterwards.

* * *

At the end of Mass, Jim the organist has played the first few notes of the hymn when, to everyone's surprise, Fr Crane comes in from the sacristy and stands near Fr Joe. He signals to Jim to stop playing.

Fr Crane has never done such a thing before. Except when he's actually saying Mass, he normally keeps out of sight as much as possible. Now he coughs nervously and begins to speak.

'Good morning, everybody', he says, and when we've all responded like good children, he goes on very shyly, 'Father Joseph thinks I should tell you that today is my Silver Jubilee.'

Before he can go on there's a burst of spontaneous clapping which everyone joins in. Fr Crane is red in the face now, and smiling, but he holds up his hand for silence and says, 'I would love to celebrate it with as many of you as can manage it. There's coffee and squash and biscuits and cake in the presbytery, so if you'd like to come, you'll be very welcome. I'll see you at the front door.' With that he vanishes as quickly as he had appeared, through the sacristy and into his house.

Meanwhile, Jim strikes up the last song again. It is 'Go, the Mass is ended.'

I always go out as quickly as I can so as to get home to Vincent. On Sundays Father Joe waits outside the church door to greet people as they come out and I see that there's only one person ahead already speaking to him and that's Jessie.

Do I try to listen to what she's saying? Do I try

not to listen? Either way, I do hear her say. 'Goodbye, Father. I'm going back to college on the afternoon train. And – thanks for everything.'

He takes her hand and shakes it. 'Thank you, Jessie,' he says 'Good luck and God bless.' She walks quickly away and he gazes after her, not seeing me. Then he pulls himself together. 'Hullo, Mary,' he says, 'tell me, is Vincent any better?'

Just then Fr Crane appears at the presbytery door, looking less nervous now he can see a crowd of people answering his invitation. Father Joe walks over to him and puts an arm across his shoulder. They are both smiling and it seems to me that the older priest is as near to being happy as I have ever seen him.

It is Fr Crane who calls across to me. 'Mary, my dear,' he says, 'I do hope you will come and join us.' I look at them both. For a brief moment I think of my Jenny, then of Jessie, and I feel deeply moved by the frailty of humanity, men and women, priests and people.

I hesitate.

Should I go into the presbytery and celebrate with my community?

Or should I go home to Vin?

Mary Brown at a Baptism

When Frank and Judy told me that they were having their baby daughter, three weeks old and as yet without a name, baptised in our church, St Teresa's, I was absolutely delighted and hugged them both.

Later I asked myself why I was so pleased. After all, we don't believe there's such a place as Limbo any more, and I'm certain that God won't love this little grandchild any more than he loves the others who are not baptised.

There's Charlie, James and Fiona's son, who by his parents' wish is to wait until he's old enough to decide for himself; there's Toby and Matt who had a New Age Naming ceremony in a meadow; and there's Beth, whose father and mother were not allowed to have her baptised.

I suppose there's a bit of me that believes that I am a failure in all this. Four out of five of my grandchildren unbaptised is a pretty poor showing, and I'm afraid some of the parishioners may pity me for this. But I think the main reason why I'm so happy about Frank and Judy's little daughter, is that baptism surely means that there will be solemn promises to bring her up a Catholic. In fact I've now reached the stage where I will be more than grateful if any of my grandchildren are brought up to believe in God, to be Christian, and it doesn't matter to me any more in which particular tradition. And yet, even so, I was very pleased, and so was Vincent, to hear that the new baby was to be 'done properly'.

I asked Judy about her name, but she told me that they hadn't decided yet. They were waiting to choose a name that suited the baby's personality. I managed to stop myself from saying that I didn't think people have developed much personality at the age of three or four weeks.

I asked Frank about the godparents. One was to be Veronica O'Grady, a sister of one of Frank's old school friends, a very nice girl and a good Catholic. But I couldn't help feeling a bit dismayed when he told me who the other two were – Jake and Audrey Weston, an attractive young couple admittedly, but not Christians of any sort. I dared to ask Frank:

'Do you think they're really suitable as godparents? Do they believe in God?' He had the grace to look just a little embarrassed.

'Well, I don't know, Mum. I don't think the subject's come up, actually. But they're great friends and nice people and I know they'll take an interest in our baby. They already have.'

I sighed. 'Well, at least you'll have Veronica,' I

said, 'and you two of course, to make sure she understands the faith.' Frank gave me a hug and chuckled.

'Mum, in some ways you're so old fashioned!' he said.

So I told myself I should be thankful. I remembered how disappointed I was when Fr Joe, of all people, who is always so pleasant and obliging, refused to baptise Beth, Peter and Susan's little girl. He said it was because they never went to church and because they wouldn't promise to bring her up a Catholic. At first I was very hurt, but when I thought it over I realised he was right. It made Susan very angry though, and I understood that too.

Then there was the 'christening' of Anne and Rex's sons, Matthew and Toby, poor little Toby with his disfigured face. They are such a dear family, so happy and carefree. I had very mixed feelings about the ceremony; I even wondered whether we should go at all, but we did, Vin and I, and I can't deny it was a joyful and memorable occasion.

We all went into the country, one sunny day towards the end of May. We parked the cars in a farmyard belonging to one of Rex's friends and walked through a meadow full of wild flowers to a stream at the edge of a little wood.

As well as our family, there were lots of Anne and

Rex's young friends, the women in pretty dresses and wearing flowers in their hair. Rex's parents were both dead and Vincent felt we should be there, I suppose to represent the older generation.

As we trooped down the hill, someone played the Pan pipes and when we got to the bottom one of Rex's friends sang something from Shakespeare, I think it was 'hey, nonny no'. We all gathered round a silver birch tree and a tall lad called Paul took Beth in his arms (she was nearly a year old then) and spoke loud and clear into the silence. He said simply, 'Little one, I name you Beth.' Then everyone clapped and laughed and there was more singing. Someone put a daisy chain round Beth's neck and we all joined hands and danced in a circle. Then some of the young women laid a big cloth on the grass and we had a grand picnic.

Afterwards, Vin said, 'It wasn't a baptism, Mary. They didn't mention God once.'

'I know, Vin,' I said. 'I'm sad about it too. But I have to admit, I enjoyed it.'

Father Joe told me he would love to baptise Frank and Judy's baby during Mass, because then she could be properly welcomed into the community. 'That's how it should be, Mary,' he said. I agreed that this would be good idea, but when I mentioned it to Judy, she said, 'Oh no, Mary, definitely not. We don't want a whole lot of strangers at our baby's baptism.'

I knew better than to argue, and the baptism was fixed for a Sunday afternoon in June, when the baby, still nameless, would be six weeks old.

* * *

It's the day of the baptism. I am relieved and grateful that we're going to Judy's parents' house afterwards. I know Vincent isn't really up to coping with a lot of people and in any case their house is much bigger than ours. Judy told me her mother is having caterers in to do the tea and this struck me as being a bit 'over the top' but of course I didn't say so.

I'm so glad it's a sunny day and warm too. I got myself a new dress from one of the charity shops in town because I realise it's going to be quite a social occasion, as well as a religious one.

We're inside St Teresa's now, all standing round the font, waiting for Fr Joe. All our family is here, except Johnny who hasn't been home for two years although he lives in the same town, and Peter and Susan and little Beth. I can understand why they didn't come. I don't think either Peter or Susan has been to church since they were not allowed to have Beth baptised, not that they went much before.

Although I have so many of my family round me today, I can't help feeling sad. Johnny is such a worry and I do miss Peter and Susan and especially Beth. I hardly ever see her nowadays, although they only live twenty miles away.

At least Anne and Rex and their little boys are here. I was afraid they wouldn't come, either, as they are both agnostics now. But when I spoke to Anne on the phone, she said,

'Of course we'll come, Mum, we'd love to. The family means a lot to us.'

She has always been such a good daughter, and I just wish — but it's her life and it's how she wants to be. Jenny is here too. She's come all the way from London and I must be thankful for that and not mind how she looks. It seems so strange to me, to wear all that black to a baptism in the middle of summer. Her mini-skirt is surely no bigger than a handkerchief and she has a stud in her nose and two rings in one eyebrow. I tell myself firmly that these things are not important.

It's the baby, of course, who is the star attraction, and so she should be. She's lying fast asleep in her carrycot, wearing the most beautiful christening gown I have ever seen. Judy's mother, Kathleen, comes across.

'Do you like the gown, Mary?' she asks.

'It's exquisite!' I say.

'It was made by Judy's great-grandmother,' Kathleen says. 'My mother wore it for her christening, I wore it for mine, and so did Judy, and now it's this little one's turn. By the way, do you know what they are going to call her?'

I shake my head. 'No, it's a big secret,' I say, 'we'll have to be patient!'

I like Kathleen. Vincent thinks she a bit worldly, and perhaps she is, but she's warm-hearted and I like her.

But here comes Fr Joe now – oh no, it's not Fr Joe, it's Father Crane. Oh dear, I can't help feeling disappointed and I know Frank will be too, because Joe is a good friend. But then I feel rather ashamed because Father Crane will do the baptism very well. We are lucky to have two such good priests.

He apologises as he approaches the font, and tells us that Fr Joe has been called away to a dying parishioner. I realise that the poor man must know how much less popular he is than the younger priest, and I feel sorry for him.

There are several little cousins in the church but they are behaving surprisingly well and everything is going smoothly until Father Crane asks for the name of the child and Frank answers in his clear voice:

'Sunshine Kathleen Mary.'

Father Crane blinks and clears his throat.

'I'm sorry, could you say that again?'

'Sunshine,' says Frank, 'Sunshine Kathleen Mary.'

There are one or two giggles and then, to my consternation, Vincent speaks up.

'You can't do that, son,' he says, 'you can't call a baby "Sunshine!"'

Frank just smiles and shrugs.

'Sorry, Dad,' he says, 'it's the name we've chosen.'

Father Crane is continuing with the baptism, very carefully pouring water from the font over the baby's head. He seems quite unaware of anything being out of the ordinary.

'I baptise you, Sunshine Kathleen Mary, in the name of the Father, and of the Son and of the Holy Spirit,' he says.

Afterwards, at Judy's parents' house, there is a grand feast: vol-au-vents, sausage rolls, trifle and meringues, not to mention champagne. I try to help Kathleen, but she asks me to sit down. Then she says, 'I'm so sorry, about the name. I mean, isn't it awful?' I hesitate and before I can answer, Judy speaks up.

'Oh Mummy, how can you say that?' she says.

'Frank and I think Sunshine is a beautiful name and it suits her perfectly. Anyway, I thought you would both be pleased. She's called Kathleen Mary after her two grannies.'

* * *

Vincent calmed down after a few weeks and we all got used to Sunshine's name. Judy was right, it does suit her. She's a happy little thing, with a sunny disposition. Vincent dotes on her

Her godparents, Jake and Audrey, are very good to her. They have no children of their own and they take a great interest in Sunshine, giving her all sorts of lovely presents.

But I am so glad of Veronica; I'm counting on her to look after Sunshine.

Mary Brown goes to Confession

I really hate it here. Oh, I know I shouldn't say that, even to myself, not when I'm in church. But it's brought it all back, how it was in the old days when I was young and going to confession every fortnight, sometimes every week.

I don't know what I'm doing here, now, at my age, when I haven't been to confession for at least three years. And yet, of course, I do know, I know exactly why I'm here. It's because of Father Joe and what he said at Mass last Sunday. He's such a nice fellow and he tries so hard, so when he asked us – well he was almost begging us – to go to confession, I thought, well, it won't hurt for once.

But the trouble is, it does hurt. It hurts because it feels all wrong. Oh, I know when I was listening to Father Joe he more or less convinced me of the great value of the Sacrament of Reconciliation, but I'm far from convinced right now, sitting in this cold, dark church – well I know it's sensible to save on heating and light but a little comfort might help – and feeling nervous and frightened just like I did every time, ever since I was a little girl. I always got that pain in my stomach and I've got it now.

I wonder if the others feel the same. There are

only four of them ahead of me now. There's old Sister Stephen from the convent – well, you'd expect her to be here, poor old thing – and little Jimmy Dooley looking mutinous and not in the least repentant. His mother must have made him come.

And then there's Winnie Searby. I know for a fact that she comes every week, has done all her life. I wonder what sins she confesses? I know it's nothing to do with me, but I'd bet anything she has a whole list of silly things she thinks are sins that she'll rattle off to Father, and she'll never ever tell him how she loves to gossip and ruin people's characters because she doesn't realise she's doing it. Winnie Searby doesn't even know herself. Oh well, she's gone in now. The rest of us had better resign ourselves to a long wait.

There's a man on the bench in front of me. I don't think he belongs to our parish. I've never seen him before. He's kneeling, with his head bowed. Perhaps he's done something really serious ...

Somebody – perhaps it's the Holy Spirit? – gives me a shake. Mary Brown, what are you thinking of? Sitting here, thinking about everyone else's sins, making judgements. You say Winnie doesn't know herself. Do you?

I slide to my knees and cover my face with my hands and close my eyes. I think I know myself, a little bit. I know I'm not a great sinner, at least not nowadays. For one thing I'm too busy just getting by, without going off the rails and committing murder or adultery. But on the other hand, I have to admit that I don't think about my sins as much as used to, or even in the way I used to.

It's partly because of the talk I heard a few weeks ago at the convent. It was on Ignatian Spirituality, and my friend, Peg, persuaded me to go with her. We learnt about this examen, which seems to me a much better idea than the examination of conscience. There's something a bit grim, as I see it now, about dwelling on your sins at the end of a full and tiring day. In the examen you go through the day remembering the good things, the high points, as well as the bad, and somehow, I suppose because you're consciously doing it before God, you can see where you've gone wrong. But you can also see your gifts and blessings. Still, today is different. I must try to see myself clearly, to realise when and how much I have failed to love God and other people. Because that's what it boils down to in the end, after all.

I hear the creak of the confessional door and open my eyes to see Winnie emerge with folded hands and downcast eyes. The little lad Jimmy makes his reluctant way towards the door she has left open.

I feel very sorry for him. I remember so clearly what it was like when I was his age.

I was frightened of the dark, uncomfortable space where I had to kneel, and the voice-without-a face of the priest, sometimes kindly, more often stern. Most of all I was afraid of confessing 'impure thoughts'. The guilt and embarrassment associated with this particular sin was so great that such thoughts and images forced themselves into my mind in spite of all my efforts. But it did happen that sometimes, when the confessor was especially kind and compassionate, I remembered that God was forgiving me and I came away feeling not just relieved that the ordeal was over, but grateful and at peace.

Here comes young Jimmy now. That was quick! He runs down the aisle, forgetting to genuflect, and if he had a penance, forgetting that too. Sister Stephen has gone in and there's only the stranger and me left. I must really try to concentrate.

I think about God first. I realise that if I really tried I could make some time in my day to be alone with him. I also realise that I hardly ever say thank you to God. I know I have plenty of troubles and worries, but I have hundreds, thousands of blessings too. And although I love Vincent more than I could ever make anyone understand, and spend so much time thinking of ways to help him now that he is so depressed, it could be that I don't give him enough space. And am I fair to my children? I sigh. I certainly have plenty to confess, and it occurs to me that I need someone wiser than me, someone who will really listen to me, to advise me on some things.

The old nun hobbles out. The stranger takes her place. It's my turn next, and I think I'll go home. I don't really feel that confession is right for me just now. I know it might be arrogant, but I don't think I need the Sacrament of Reconciliation any more.

I know that God loves me. I believe this with all my heart. I think of him as my Father and myself as his child. I am sure that when I am truly sorry for the mistakes I have made and the things I have deliberately done wrong, my Father will forgive me instantly and completely. My sins that were as scarlet will be whiter than snow. I understand this because it's been the same with me and my children. If ever they say 'sorry' and mean it, I forgive them at once. So it's not difficult for me to trust in God in this way. I don't need the mumbo-jumbo of confession. I don't need a priest as 'intermediary', because I neither need nor want an intermediary. I just want God to forgive me.

This has been a dreadful mistake. I'm just wasting my time and I'll be wasting Fr Joe's time too if I go through with it. I'm going home.

I stand up and move into the aisle. As I genuflect, I hear the door of the confessional open again. I turn to walk out of the church and home to Vincent. And then, I shall never know why, I turn round and walk towards the confessional. As soon as I'm through the door all the old feelings of anxiety and dread come flooding back. I'm beginning to lower myself onto the kneeler when from the other side of the grille, Father Joe speaks.

'If you'd like to come round where we can see each other, you're welcome,' he says.

I hesitate. I feel it will be even more embarrassing to have to face the priest, but I've always hated the cramped little box, so I walk round a screen and there's Father Joe, sitting in an armchair.

To my surprise, his face lights up when he sees me. He gets to his feet and shakes my hand.

' Hello, Mary!' he says, 'It's good to see you.'

He invites me to sit down and asks after Vincent. Then he says

'You're not nervous, Mary, are you?'

'Well, yes, I am a bit,' I say, 'I've never been to face-to-face confession before.'

He laughs.

'But we're old friends, aren't we?' he says. After that, it gets easier. I tell him my sins, and somehow, without realising it, I'm telling him my troubles too, I'm telling him what my life is really like. I don't think I've said so much to anyone for years.

Father Joe stands up and places his hands on my head as he gives me absolution. He says something about God's unfailing mercy and unconditional love and he asks me to pray for him.

'I will, Father,' I say, 'I already do. But what about my penance?'

He laughs. 'Mary, I forgot,' he says. 'now let me think about what you've told me and see if I can come up with a suitable penance.' After a moment he says,

'Right. For your penance I'd like you to meditate on Psalm 62, the first three verses. I've listened carefully to what you have told me, and I think it might be worth asking yourself the question, 'Where is the centre of my life?' I think it might be a good idea to read this psalm slowly and prayerfully, perhaps two or three times, letting the words really sink in.

He smiles. 'God bless you, Mary, and thank you for coming. I will be praying for you.'

I walk home feeling happy and at peace. But

then I think: how many people are lucky enough to find a confessor like Father Joe?

Later that evening I take out my bible and find the psalm.

> O God, you are my God, for you I long;
> for you my soul is thirsting,
> my body pines for you
> like a dry, weary land without water.
> So I gaze on you in the sanctuary
> to see your strength and your glory.
>
> For your love is better than life,
> my lips will speak your praise.
> So I will bless you all my life,
> in your name I will lift up my hands.
> My soul shall be filled as with a banquet,
> my mouth shall praise you with joy.
>
> On my bed I remember you.
> On you I muse through the night
> for you have been my help;
> in the shadow of your wings I rejoice.
> My soul clings to you;
> your right hand hold me fast.

I think I understand why Father Joe gave me this penance.

Mary Brown and the Eucharist

Last Thursday, I felt very hurt, hurt and angry and upset.

The day began so well. It was warm and sunny as I set out to call for Dorothy. She is one of my best friends, an Anglican and a good woman. She seems to me to have just the right balance between being prayerful yet also deeply involved in service to others. Among other things she does voluntary work at the hospice and with the disabled and she also writes prayers and poems which never fail to move me.

I had heard that there was going to be a Quiet Day at St Brigid's Convent, led by a Dominican priest who was said to be both a skilled retreat-giver and a nice man. The theme of the day was taken from St John's First Letter: 'My dear people, let us love one another.'

The convent is a pleasant building and the large walled garden is well tended. I was sure that it was just the sort of day that Dorothy would appreciate. But when I invited her to come with me, she hesitated for a moment.

'Will I be the only one there who isn't a Roman Catholic?' she asked.

'I'm not sure,' I said, 'but I can guarantee you'll

be very welcome. The sisters are very open-minded and very enthusiastic about Christian Unity.'

So Dorothy agreed to come and the nuns were as friendly and warm towards her as I could have wished. The Dominican, Father Michael, was everything people had said about him. He had the rare gift of being both simple and profound, so that I could easily understand everything he said (and this is not always the case for me). I was also aware of being led into new insights.

There was also plenty of silence, which I knew Dorothy values, and we were allowed to wander where we liked in the beautiful garden. The nuns provided us with a light but delicious lunch, and although we felt sleepy afterwards, Father Michael woke us all up with an amusing talk.

The day was to end with Mass at four o'clock and we all helped to prepare it. We chose the readings ourselves and one of the women made a beautiful arrangement with flowers from the convent garden and some symbols of love. One of the younger sisters plays the guitar well and she offered to accompany the singing. Others put together an interesting collage, illustrating different ways of loving.

Dorothy and I were invited to take up the bread and wine at the offertory and she seemed pleased to have been asked. A few minutes before the start of Mass, as we were walking together towards the chapel, she said,

'Mary, I can't tell you how grateful I am that you've brought me here today. It's been just perfect. I really liked Father Michael; he's such a good teacher, and the place is delightful – not to mention the weather – but what I appreciate most is the way I've been welcomed and accepted, the way it has made me feel that I belong to this family of God. I feel that we truly are all one.'

I was going to reply to this but Dorothy caught sight of Father Michael, also making his way to the chapel.

'Hang on a minute, Mary,' she said, 'I'll just check that it's all right for me to receive communion.'

I stayed where I was, watching her hurrying, so cheerful and confident across the grass, and I felt uneasy. I felt worse when I saw her face as she walked slowly back to me.

'He said No,' she said, simply, sadly. She looked at me and added, 'he said if I cross my arms like this when I approach him I may receive a blessing. I don't think I want a blessing.'

I walked into the chapel with Dorothy and we sat together at the back. We made all the responses and joined in the singing. We took up the offerings together and I saw that like me, Dorothy smiled at the priest as she handed him the hosts. When it came time for communion, everyone else in the chapel went up to receive the body and blood of Our Lord, everyone that is except Dorothy, and me.

There was a period of quiet during which I tried to untangle my feelings. I felt anger and hurt, I felt upset for Dorothy, but I also felt a certain guilt. After all, who am I to refuse Jesus when he invites me to the eucharist?

People were singing now, softly:
'This is my body
broken for you.
Take it and eat it,
and when you do,
do it in love for me.'

But I didn't. I refused to take and eat, and I did it in love for Dorothy, my friend. I wondered, as I have wondered so often, what God our all-loving Father, thinks about all this. As I said, it has left me feeling hurt and angry and upset.

A day or two later I was still worrying about what happened, so I decided to go round to see Fr Joe. I told him the whole story and as always, he listened attentively.

When I'd finished, he thought for a while, then said:

'That's a sad story, Mary, and I can guess how you feel. But it's a pity, because I'm sure the Quiet Day at the convent would have counted as a special, private occasion, when your Anglican friend should have been allowed to receive communion.'

But I found no comfort in this.

'How can that be right, Father?' I asked. 'Surely it's either right or it's wrong, whether it's special and private or not?'

He smiled at me.

'I can see you're becoming quite a rebel, Mary,' he said, almost as though he was paying me a compliment, and he went on to say,

'I sympathise with everything you've said, especially as I've met Dorothy more than once and I'm sure she's a sensitive and holy woman. And I also sympathise with your reaction. But we belong to this club, called the Roman Catholic Church, and we have to keep to the rules even when to us they seem idiotic or, as in this case, positively perverse.'

I'm afraid Fr Joe didn't succeed in convincing me, even when he added,

'And in any case, from what I know of your friend, Dorothy, she has a big enough heart not to hold it against us.'

Since then I've been thinking a lot about the eucharist. I remember how I felt that day with Dorothy when I refused to receive Our Lord. I remember the strange, cold, empty feeling of deprivation that came over me. And I think of all those others, even within the fold of our church, who are denied or deny themselves holy communion, the gift of Jesus himself.

I think of those who are divorced, sometimes through no fault of their own, and have found a loving enriching relationship with someone new which prohibits them from receiving communion. And I also think of the people who think of themselves as being in a state of grave sin, and cannot bring themselves to repent, or perhaps forgive themselves. And then there are the ones who feel themselves to be unfit to receive the body and blood of Our Lord, as though any of us is 'worthy'. It seems so sad that all of these people are unable, for one reason or another, to receive this life-giving sacrament.

* * *

This morning I received a note from Sister Agnes at the convent, telling me about a Quiet Day to be held next month. The theme is 'Reconciliation'. I wonder if I'll dare to invite Dorothy?

Mary Brown and Confirmation

I'm sitting up in the gallery at St Teresa's, in the front row where I can have the best view of what's happening down in the church. There are eleven candidates for confirmation and they are all there already, each sitting next to his or her sponsor in the two front rows. Even from up here I can see that they are all dressed in their best clothes, and they're not talking or even whispering.

I can't help feeling a glow of pride. I'm not related to any of these children, but this time I did have a small part to play in preparing them for today. One day a few months ago Fr Crane asked me to come to see him, and when I did he asked me if I would be one of the team helping to prepare the children for confirmation.

I was dismayed. I don't like to refuse a priest anything, especially one as considerate as Fr Crane, but I felt completely out of my depth here.

'Oh, Father,' I said, 'I'm sorry but I just can't. I can't teach and I don't know nearly enough …'

I stopped because I could see he was laughing.

'No, no, Mary,' he said, 'I'm not asking you to teach anybody. But you see, this time we're inviting the parents to come along with the children, and what we need is people like you and Jean – she's already said yes – to be a sort of sympathetic presence, to talk with the parents and to listen to them during the tea break, to put them at their ease, that sort of thing.'

I felt flattered, and I thought this might be something I could do, so rather nervously, I agreed.

The classes were held on Friday nights in the primary school, which is next to the church. The teacher was Miss Grimshaw, someone who taught all my children at school, someone I admire very much. I will always be grateful for the way she encouraged Peter, who was slightly dyslexic. I feel sure he wouldn't have persevered, and eventually got himself to university, if it hadn't been for Miss Grimshaw. She is quite old now, near to retiring I think, and I thought how good it was of her to give up her time for this class after teaching all week.

The lessons were fascinating and I found I was learning a lot myself. But what I liked best was the tea break, when the children went off to another room and we talked with the mothers (and one father who bravely came along to the class). I have made one or two new friends on these Friday nights and I've discovered a lot about the lives some people live, lives so different from mine.

Two of the families come from Greenlands, the notorious council estate on the edge of town which is anything but green. It's the sort of place where old people don't dare to go out at night and where vandalism and drugs are rife. Sadly for us, it's where our Johnny sleeps on a mate's floor.

Vincent and I don't have much money. We used up his redundancy pay long ago and after the last of the children left home we moved into a small terrace house in the old part of town. It's a bit shabby, but I realise now that it's luxury compared with a high rise flat on the Greenlands estate. I would come home on Friday nights quite dizzy with everything I had learnt about God from Miss Grimshaw, and about life on the estate from Betty and Diane.

On the very first evening I had agreed to act as sponsor to Diane's son Jason, an undersized little boy, who, I privately thought, was far too immature to be getting confirmed. He was quiet and withdrawn, the opposite of his mother, the noisiest and most talkative woman in the room. It took several Friday nights before Jason would speak to me.

Jean particularly befriended Betty, a big, untidy young woman with dyed blond hair who kept nipping out for a smoke and was usually five or ten minutes late. However she did, eventually, turn up every Friday night with her daughter Cindy, who seemed like an exact replica of her mother, except that her hair was naturally blond. Cindy happened to have a particularly low, pleasant voice and I was so pleased when Miss Grimshaw chose her to be the one who would read the epistle at the confirmation Mass. It was lovely to see Cindy's normally expressionless face brighten. I guessed that this child wasn't very often chosen for anything at all.

I felt quite low as I walked towards the school on the last Friday. I realised how much I had benefited from the lessons with Miss Grimshaw and I hoped I wouldn't lose touch with Betty and Diane.

The lesson was going smoothly as always when, half an hour late, in came Betty and Cindy. I saw at once that Betty had been crying but Miss Grimshaw didn't seem to notice this. She spoke very coldly: 'Mrs Fowler,' she said, 'You have exhausted my patience. This must be the fourth or fifth time you have brought Cindy here late, and tonight we are half an hour into this very important final lesson before you condescend to turn up! Cindy does not deserve to read the epistle on Sunday, if you can't even take the trouble to get her here on time, so I shall choose someone else to take her place.'

I suppose most of us felt like schoolchildren

again, quaking in silence. But not Diane. She stood up, scraping back her chair.

'You old cow!' she shouted at Miss Grimshaw, 'you think you're so clever, spoutin' all that stuff! But you don't know nothin'! You ain't taken the trouble to get to know us, to get to know what's goin' on in our lives. You ain't got a clue!' The scorn in her voice was frightening. She paused for a minute and then went on.

'You didn't know did you, that Betty 'ere gets beat up most Friday nights when she gets 'ome from your class. You didn't know that 'e left 'er for good this dinnertime? You 'aven't an idea what it's like to be 'er, 'ave you? Well, you can stuff your confirmation lessons as far as I'm concerned. I'm off and you won't see sight nor sound of our Jason on Sunday.' She grabbed Jason by the hand and was turning to go when Miss Grimshaw spoke.

'Please, Mrs Fletcher, just wait a moment. I am so very sorry. You are quite right in everything you say. I haven't got to know you as people, I don't know what it's like to live like that. And in any case, I shouldn't have taken it out on Cindy. None of this is her fault. Look, Mrs Fletcher,' she said, and she was pleading now, 'it doesn't matter if you can't accept my apology. But please, don't let it stop Jason from being confirmed. I would be very unhappy if that happened.'

But Diane's face was unrelenting. 'So what?' she shouted, 'I should care if you're unhappy! It's about time you had a taste of it!' She turned and strode out of the room, dragging Jason with her.

* * *

This morning I sigh, re-living that nightmare scene. I felt so sorry both for Betty and for Miss Grimshaw. But at least today everything is looking good, everything except the absence of Jason. Cindy's blond hair is shining; she sits at the end of the row next to her sponsor, Jean, ready to get up and walk out to read the epistle.

She is actually in the middle of reading it, and reading very well, when the commotion starts. A tall redhead is striding down the aisle towards the front, her heels clicking on the hard floor, hand in hand with a young boy. Diane! Jason! And I'm his sponsor! In a panic I scramble out of the pew, run down the stairs from the gallery and into the church. Several people are standing at the back as the church is full. I push my way through, breathing hard, and stop. A slim figure, dressed in grey, has slipped out of a pew near the front. She looks at Diane who nods and lets her take Jason's hand. Then Miss Grimshaw leads him to join the others and sits next to him. I retreat to my place in the gallery, too relieved and happy to feel foolish.

When it comes to the actual confirmation, the old bishop speaks each candidate's name clearly. When he reaches the last child, Jason Fletcher, and I hear his new name, 'Bruno', there are tears in my eyes.

I still wonder if Jason Bruno and his friends aren't too young to be confirmed. In early adolescence everything is confusing and uncertain. Couldn't they make a truer, firmer commitment a few years later? But I suppose the church knows best … Sometimes I can't help wondering.

Mary Brown and Marriage

Vincent and I were absolutely stunned by Jenny's telephone call. We simply couldn't believe it.

She had phoned one evening out of the blue to tell us that she is getting married to a wonderful man called Hugh.

'You'll be happy to know he's a Catholic, Mum,' she said, 'and we'd like to get married in St Teresa's.'

Jenny marrying a Catholic! We were astonished because she, of all our children, was the most fiercely anti-Catholic and unconventional in every way. It seemed incredible that she would want to be married in church.

Of course, the news made us very happy. None of the others had been married in St Teresa's. Frank and Judy were the only ones who had a Catholic wedding which took place in her church. It was very formal and quite quick because there was no Mass, and the photographs afterwards took much longer than the service itself. The priest was new to the parish and didn't know either Judy or Frank, which made the whole thing seem rather impersonal.

Cathy, our eldest daughter, isn't married; she lives with her Indian friend Shanti. Peter and Susan are not married, nor are Anne and Rex. James and

Fiona were married in the Methodist church, and though I have never admitted this, even to Vin, theirs was the wedding I liked best.

And now it will be Jenny's turn, Jenny who not so long ago had an abortion, who openly scorned the church's teaching on almost everything, who was an ardent feminist, who scoffed at marriage, and priests and nuns … Jenny whom we loved and came near to despairing of. I suppose that together with Johnny, I thought of her as our failure. Jenny is pretty, beautiful even, and I suppose she is charming. She has been to drama school and had one or two small parts on television. She's gone through lots of boyfriends but as far as we know, had no serious relationships. And now this: marriage, and to a Catholic!

I think quite a lot about marriage. I am very much aware that my own experience has been good, that in spite of difficult times and considerable problems of one sort or another, Vincent and I are very blessed in one another. I think this is partly because each of us puts the other's happiness first. And of course it helps that God is so real to both of us.

I realise that married life is not so easy for a great many people. My sister, Bernadette, has just left her husband after thirty-five years of marriage. I was very shocked when I heard about it, and at first I felt very sorry for Sidney, her husband. But Bernie came to stay with us and when she described what marriage to Sidney was like, I was surprised that she'd stayed with him so long. On the other hand, it does seem that some couples give up too easily when the going gets tough. Yet none of us really knows what anyone else's marriage is really like, and probably we are much too quick to make judgements.

When I've talked about it with Peter and Susan and Anne and Rex, both couples say the same thing. They believe that the important thing is to have a true and lasting commitment, and they claim that they can have this without a church service or a piece of paper certifying that they are man and wife.

I once asked Anne if Toby and Matt might not feel uncomfortably different because their parents are not married. She told me that in Matt's class of thirty children only three of them have married parents, and it is those three that are looked upon as the odd ones. And Peter told me about two couples he knows. They each lived together for several years, then decided to get married. Within three years, in both cases, the couples were seeking a divorce.

For someone like me, this is all distressing and

confusing, although I have to admit that both Peter and Susan and Anne and Rex seem very happy and loving in their relationships. Like Vin and me, they were all very surprised to hear Jenny's news.

Soon after her phone call, she brought Hugh home to meet us. At first, my feelings about him were mixed. I saw a nice-looking young man who quite clearly adored Jenny. He was courteous and well-mannered and from his conversation I realised he was highly intelligent. He got on well with Vin from the first; they have a love of cricket and rugby in common. Hugh works as a barrister in London and he already has a flat where he and Jenny can live when they are married, so there were no worries on that score.

What did worry me though, is the difference in social class. It was quite obvious that Hugh came from a completely different background from ours, and I wondered how Jenny would fit in with his family.

After supper Vin took Hugh down to the pub. Jenny and I made another cup of tea and sat together by the fire. She looked lovely, and so different from the way she was, not so long ago, at Sunshine's baptism. Now her hair was cut very short and she wore very little make-up. Best of all she seemed serenely happy.

'Now, Mum, tell me what you think of Hugh,' she said.

'Well,' I began carefully, 'he's a very nice young man ...'

Jenny picked up my hesitation.

'But?' she said.

'But, well, oh Jen, I don't know how to put this, but he's ...'

'Oh, Mum!' said Jenny, laughing, 'you mean he's posh!'

I laughed too, relieved that she'd said it.

'Well, yes, I'm afraid he's out of our class. I just think it might be difficult for you to fit in with those sort of people,' I said tamely.

'Mum,' said Jenny firmly, 'do you know you're a snob, what's called an inverted snob? And as a good Catholic, you ought not to be!'

I suppose I should have felt affronted at Jenny of all people telling me about being a good Catholic. But I was so pleased that she was interested in anything to do with the church that I just said,

'What do you mean, Jen?'

'I mean that we are all equal in the sight of God,' said Jen, 'and that means we should treat each other as equals. Hugh's mother understands that. She welcomed me into the family with open arms, literally.'

'You've met her?' I asked, 'What's she like?'

'She's like Hugh, gentle and considerate and warm and fun. His father's nice too, but more like everyone's idea of an old fashioned, jolly lord of the manor.'

It turned out that Hugh had taken Jenny to meet his parents the previous weekend. Jenny, curled up in the big chair by the fire with her shoes kicked off and a mug of tea in her hands, told me all about it.

Lord and Lady Byland, Hugh's parents, lived in Northumberland, in a Tudor house which had belonged to his family, a recusant Catholic family, for generations. They had three sons, Hilary, Sebastian and Hugh, but no daughters. Lord Byland, who had asked Jenny to call him George, as everyone else did, was a retired army officer, and Lady Byland, Charlotte, was a doctor.

'She's lovely, Mum,' Jenny said, 'I can't wait for you two to meet. I know you'll like her. In fact, they've asked us to take you and Dad up there to meet them.'

I might have known that Vincent wouldn't come with us. I couldn't help being nervous. Hugh drove Jenny and me up to Northumberland and I could tell they were both doing their best to put me at ease. But as soon as we stepped inside the gracious old building my anxiety fell away. A slender, grey-haired woman about my own age came forward and greeted me warmly, and her large, red-faced husband clasped my hand in both his huge ones and said how glad they were to welcome me. He spoke with such obvious sincerity that I abandoned my foolish reservations there and then.

It was a weekend I shall never forget. It was such a joy to stay in that wonderful old house with those kindly people, and my only disappointment was that Vincent wasn't there with me.

On the Saturday afternoon I went for a walk through the woods on the estate with Charlotte. We talked, and in the talking became friends. I had been envying her what seemed from the outside to be a perfect life, but she told me that she had just been diagnosed as having multiple sclerosis, that her son Hilary was an alcoholic and Sebastian had been unable to hold down any job. I told her about Vincent's depression and Johnny's involvement in drugs and poor Toby's scarred face. But we also shared the many joys in both our lives and laughed a lot. By Sunday I had completely forgotten that this family was 'posh'.

On Sunday morning we had Mass in the old chapel which was only a short distance from the house. Inside it was quite beautiful, built of warm golden-coloured stone, with graceful arches and slender pillars. It was also surprisingly light and airy for such an old church and sunshine came flooding in as we celebrated Mass. The congregation came from two nearby villages and the priest was 'on loan' from a seminary not far away.

'We never know who it will be,' said George 'it's rather fun!' I noticed how he always seemed to look on the bright side.

As we came out, Jenny said to me, 'Isn't it lovely?'

'It's perfect,' I answered, and then I saw the look on her face. She blushed.

'I couldn't ask you, Mum. I know St Teresa's means so much to you.'

I thought, it's so wonderful that Jenny's returned to the faith, it's so wonderful that she and Hugh are so happy together, what does it matter where we have the wedding? I smiled at her, 'Well, I'll leave it to you to persuade your father.'

* * *

This is a fairytale wedding. I can't believe it isn't just a beautiful dream. Everything is perfect, well almost. The sun is shining; the little churchyard is full of wild daffodils. Father Joe is here. Jenny persuaded him to come and marry them and as there isn't a permanent priest here it wasn't too difficult to arrange. All our children and grandchildren are with us, all except Johnny which is why it isn't quite perfect.

Hugh stands at the front with his brother Hilary. In the past few months I have grown very fond of him. All at once the organist, who was playing softly, swings into a joyous piece by Bach which Charlotte had chosen, and Jenny, wearing a simple white dress comes into the church on Vincent's arm. I have never seen him look so proud and both of them are beaming. Beth and little Sunshine, dressed in pretty cotton frocks, come skipping along behind.

Jenny and Hugh have planned this wedding with Fr Joe, down to the last detail: the music, the songs, the flowers, the prayers, the readings. For me it all passes in a joyous blur, until it comes to the sign of peace when Hugh and Jenny come round to us all and, suddenly and spontaneously, everyone in the old church – even Vincent – is hugging everyone else!

A long time afterwards when the splendid reception is over, I walk across to the church again. Father Joe is there, kneeling in a pew, but he doesn't notice me.

I pray with all my heart, for this marriage to last. And I pray for Johnny.

Mary Brown and Ordination

Last Saturday, my friend Clare's son Tim was ordained priest in our church. Sadly I wasn't able to go because I had promised to look after Matt and Toby for the weekend so that their parents could have a break.

But I did pray especially hard for Tim that day and I thought about him a lot. He's the same age as my Frank, and they've been friends since they were very small. Tim was often at our house and I used to notice him particularly out of all the gang of children who used to come, because he was such a lively child and full of mischief. He was a very popular boy, outgoing and friendly not only towards lads of his own age but to old people and little children as well. At one stage our youngest, Johnny, idolised Tim. And I remember as a teenager, he was a great favourite with the girls.

He doesn't seem to have changed, although he must be nearly thirty now. He had several different jobs before he went to the seminary and I believe those experiences will stand him in good stead as a priest. Because of his personality and his time working in the rough and tumble of 'real life', I think Tim stands a good chance of being a good priest, and a happy and fulfilled one. I hope so.

One of the many things I feel guilty about is that I don't pray for vocations any more, even though I know there is a shortage of priests. I used to pray most fervently, and not only for vocations in general, but in the hopes that Frank or Peter or James would receive a calling from God to be priests. Vincent and I prayed with the children every day and we tried to set an example by going to Mass as often as we could and regularly to confession. All of them went to Catholic schools, primary and secondary too, although they had to travel to the next town to get to the Catholic comprehensive and it had a poor academic reputation. All our boys served on the altar as soon as they were old enough and I remember clearly how angelic they looked and how proud I was of them all.

But somewhere along the line I seem to have changed the way I think

Over the years I have known a number of unhappy priests, and a lot of really lonely ones. I wish that priests were allowed to marry. I know that marriages are not often 'made in heaven'; they can be miserable and sometimes disastrous. I also know that there are some excellent priests who, because they are celibate, have unlimited time and energy to give to God and to their people. But even so, marriage can bring the companionship and fulfilment that is denied to so many priests, and I can't help feeling that there would be less loneliness, and perhaps less alcoholism too, if those of the clergy who wished to were permitted to marry.

I also think it's more difficult to be a priest nowadays than it was when I was young. For one thing, the people of the parish, the lay people, used to be submissive; now they are often critical and sometimes downright aggressive. I don't for a minute think that priests should be put on a pedestal or that they should act in an autocratic fashion, but I do think they should be treated with respect. I have heard too, that some priests feel vulnerable because so many cases of sexual abuse by the clergy have been uncovered. They imagine people might be suspecting them. For all these reasons, I haven't prayed for vocations among my own children, although I guess if they could be married I would be happy and proud for them to be ordained.

This ordination of Tim has set me thinking about the priests I have known. It is true that some of them have exasperated Vin and me, and some have needed our friendship and hospitality, but the ones who stand out in my memory have in their different ways inspired us, encouraged us, affirmed us and given us strength when we needed it. Some of them I count among my dearest friends.

Perhaps the most lovable of all was Father Aidan. Sadly, he died a long time ago, but I will never forget him.

Long before it was usual, he invited us to call him by his Christian name, and he was seldom to be seen wearing black. When he came to our house for a meal, he always insisted on helping with the washing up. He never forgot the children's names and took a genuine interest in each one of them.

I first knew Aidan when I was in the fifth form at school. He used to come and talk to us informally once a week. I remember he had a favourite piece of writing, 'The Rune of Hospitality', which he recited to us so often in his soft Irish brogue that I have it by heart still:

'I saw a stranger yestreen.
I put food in the eating place,
music in the listening place.
And in the sacred name of the Triune
he blessed me and my house,
my cattle and my dear ones.
And the lark said in her song:
'Often, often, often,
goes the Christ in the stranger's guise.'

Fr Aidan told us to look out for Christ in everyone we met. Still, today, I can recall him saying, 'A person does not have to be a Catholic for you to befriend and care for him or her. He doesn't have to be a Christian, he doesn't have to be religious. He might be an agnostic or an atheist, but it should make no difference. Give him what he needs of you.' Even after all this time I have remembered, and I try to live in the way the old priest (he was old even then) wanted us to live.

There was a boy in our form, Dermot, who was constantly in trouble. When he stole a big sum of money from the school secretary's office, the headmaster's patience gave out and he was expelled.

Dermot lived with his mother, stepfather and two small stepsisters. When the stepfather heard what had happened, he gave the boy a thrashing. Dermot ran away and when Father Aidan heard that he was sleeping rough he went to look for him. He took Dermot into his own home and kept him for two years.

Vin and I will always remember Aidan.

I know Tim would have had stars in his eyes on Saturday, just as most brides have stars in their eyes. But I am not idealistic enough to expect those stars to shine brightly forever! In the day-to-day reality of a priest's life, just as in the lives of us married folk, there will be bad times as well as good. Nowadays many people give up on marriage, some would say too easily. I think myself that marriage should be, wherever possible, a lifelong commitment, if only for the sake of the children, but I do wonder why this should be necessary for priests. People change, after all. I remember a priest friend – and he was a very good priest – saying in a moment of confidence, 'I'm tired of loving everybody; I just want to love one person who loves me in return.'

I know we are very blessed in our parish to have not one but two wonderful priests. I suppose it is true that Father Joe, although he is much younger, has been the 'saving' of Father Crane. He's saved him in the sense that he has helped him to become freer, more open, more confident, perhaps just to become himself.

Recently some of the initiatives in our parish have come from Father Crane. Last week he called a meeting of all the parish and gave a talk on the state of the priesthood. He was very candid and he said that he and Fr Joe need the help of us layfolk. He said how much the church had undervalued the potential of lay people, especially women, in the past, and what it comes down to is that he wants us to have a much greater share in the running of the parish, which he says, is ours not his, because he could be moved somewhere else at any time.

So that he and Fr Joe can have more time for prayer, for listening to people and visiting them, he is going to hand over all the administration and all the finance of St Teresa's to lay people to manage on his behalf. He wants us to elect a parish council and to set up groups to cover all the sorts of areas we don't yet focus on as a community – things like poverty, violence, bereavement, drugs, and literacy. It sounds like quite a grand scheme and I for one am willing to give it a try and take a part. Some people are sceptical though; they say the running of the parish will all be in the hands of a few power-seeking folk and it won't last. I disagree and I think Fr Crane (and Fr Joe of course) deserve all the support we can give them.

If Tim turns out to have anything like the calibre of these two men, or can live his life as Father Aidan lived his, then his ordination is certainly a cause for celebration.

Mary Brown and the Sacrament of Anointing

The Healing Service at St Teresa's the other Sunday afternoon was wonderful. I knew it would be, because my friend Clare had been to one led by the same priest last month, and Clare and I generally like the same things. Besides, the priest, Fr Tom Watkins, is someone Fr Joe knows well, and I know he wouldn't have encouraged me to go to the service if he hadn't every confidence in his friend.

I thought to myself, this is just what Vincent needs. Serious depression is a dreadful sickness, and he's had it for so long now. Perhaps, if he comes along to the service he will be healed at last. I began to picture how it would be, with Vin restored to his former carefree self, always ready with a joke, but I was brought back to earth with a bump when he absolutely refused to come with me.

'You know I don't like these new-fangled goings-on, Mary,' he said. 'You go if you like, but don't worry about me. I'll be better in my own good time.'

I could tell he was sorry, because he knew how disappointed I was, but I couldn't bring myself to be forgiving, not just then, because I wanted so much to help him and he was so stubborn.

Everything about the service was peaceful and gentle and reassuring. The church was more than half full, which was surprising for a Sunday afternoon. There were quite a lot of people I knew there, and a number of strangers. At the front there were several people in wheelchairs (I'm so glad we put in a ramp so that they can get in easily) and there was a mother – someone I didn't know – carrying a small white-faced bald-headed child who must, I thought, have leukaemia or some other form of cancer. There was a blind man from our parish, and I was very moved to see that old Henry Dawson, so frail himself, had brought along Elsie, who has Alzheimer's disease. I didn't know whether to pray for miracles or to hope that no-one was expecting one.

Most of the people there were like me, with nothing wrong, or rather nothing obviously physically wrong with them. When Fr Tom began to speak, he told us that most people need healing, of one sort or another. He said that there would probably be no miracles that afternoon, but that all of us, if we were open and receptive to God's love, might receive some healing of mind and spirit. Then after we had sung 'Lay your hands gently upon us' and listened to the reading from the gospels about the paralysed man who was let down through a roof, Fr Tom talked about the Sacrament of the Sick, which he said, is more properly called the Sacrament of Anointing. He explained how the priest places his finger in the holy oil and with it makes the sign of the cross on a person's forehead and hands.

He invited all those who wished to receive the sacrament to come forward. At first it didn't even occur to me to go. As far as I knew there's nothing wrong with my body, unless I count my knees and the sick headaches I keep getting. But thinking about what Fr Tom had said, I realised that I was full of anxiety, always worrying about something or other, and I thought I would, after all, go up to the altar rails where people were gathering, some kneeling, some standing.

As I waited for my turn for the priest to anoint me, I prayed hard to be like the woman in the gospels who touched the hem of Jesus's garment and was healed because of her great faith. I hoped that Jesus would say to me, 'Your faith has made you whole.'

I found it moving when Fr Tom laid his hands on my head, because it is such a nice comforting gesture. And I liked the actual anointing of my forehead and hands, and the words spoken over me:

'Through this holy anointing, may the Lord in

his love and mercy help you, with the grace of the Holy Spirit.'

As I came away I felt calm and restored and at peace and I thought, I'm glad I came.

Back at home, I described everything to Vincent and he said, 'I'm sorry. Perhaps I should have come with you, Mary.' Then he reminded me about my mother's last illness. She was living with us at the time, bedridden with cancer. The priest (it was the one before Fr Crane) visited her regularly to give her communion. One night, after she had taken the host, and was lying there, half asleep, he said,

'I'd like to give you the Sacrament of the Sick, Catherine.' To my amazement she sat bolt upright, her eyes wide with fright.

'You mean Extreme Unction, Father?' she said, speaking clearly for the first time in weeks, 'You mean I'm going to die?'

The priest tried to reassure her, tried to explain that our understanding of this sacrament has changed, that it is meant to strengthen us when we are sick. But Mother's head had fallen back on the pillow, her eyes were half closed and tears were trickling from under her eyelids.

The priest crept away and I stayed with her until she was properly asleep, thinking what a shame that she hadn't been able to understand, and more than that, what a shame that such a good woman was so afraid to die. Vincent used to say, half admiring, half joking:

'If anyone deserves a front row seat in heaven, it's your mother.'

I was thinking about heaven last week when I went to the funeral of Damian Young, a lad of twenty from our parish who was killed in a motorbike accident ten days ago. Damian was the only son of good Catholic parents, and when I went to see his mother a couple of days after the accident, she paused in her weeping to ask:

'Is there any chance he'll get to heaven, Mary? He was such a good lad …'

Damian was not a good lad, not in most people's eyes. Certainly he was not a good Catholic. I had never seen him at Mass since he was about thirteen, but I had often seen him hanging around street corners with his mates, smoking and drinking cans of beer when he should have been in school. Like Johnny, he got in with a crowd of lads older than himself, who couldn't find work and got involved in vandalism and petty thieving. I knew Damian had a police record.

However, things seemed to change for the better

when for his eighteenth birthday his parents bought him a motorbike. He went around with a different crowd now, bikers. He looked brighter and cleaner and when I met him in the street he told me he had applied for a job in a local garage. That was the nice thing about Damian – he always took the trouble to be polite and to speak even to people like me, an elderly woman who can hardly have been of any interest to him. He got the job in the garage and began to study to qualify as a mechanic. But one wet Saturday night he was riding too fast and skidded on a bend. He rode straight into a lamppost and was killed outright.

No Extreme Unction, no Sacrament of the Sick, no last minute confession for Damian. In the eyes of the church, he died in a state of sin, perhaps grave sin, as he had defied the teaching of the church for so long. But what about Damian in God's eyes? How can we know? I believe, and I wish I could persuade his mother and father to believe, that God's mercy is infinite, that he will surely take Damian to him as Mary took Jesus in her arms after he was let down from the cross, with the tenderest of love, because our God is like that.

* * *

I am thinking all this here in the church at the funeral, knowing perfectly well that a lot of my friends would disapprove of my attitude, just as they disapproved of Damian when he was alive. The church is filling up nicely. I'm pleased about that. At least Paddy and Moira will feel supported by the parish. It's what I call a black funeral. Recently I've been to one or two funerals of old people where we were asked to come in cheerful colours because the family and friends wanted the occasion to be a celebration of the dead person's life. One of my friends came to her husband's funeral smiling and wearing a dress that was patterned in all the colours of the rainbow. I admired her, but I know I could never manage that if Vincent died first.

There is a beautiful arrangement of white flowers. They are probably sweet-scented but I can only smell mothballs – there are so many men here wearing black suits that obviously don't often come out of the wardrobe. Damian's coffin stands right at the front in the middle, with a single wreath of red roses laid on the lid.

There is not much talking among the congregation, just one or two subdued murmurs, and when the organ increases its volume we all get to our feet and stand in respect as Paddy and Moira come into the church. They look so pitiful, somehow small and crumpled, though his black suit and her black coat both look new. Moira isn't actually weeping, but her face is white and set. Paddy holds her arm and they seem to be steadying each other as they make their way slowly down the aisle.

Suddenly, to my surprise, Vincent grips my arm. He's not normally a demonstrative man, certainly not in public. And I look at him anxiously. There are tears in his eyes and I know what he's thinking, because I'm thinking it too:

'There but for the grace of God …'

We begin by singing 'The Old Rugged Cross', a hymn I seem to hate and love at the same time. We are half way through when there's a noise at the back of the church and we are aware that quite a lot of people have come in. I can't resist turning round to look, and nor can most people. There's a crowd of young people, mostly boys but a few girls too, all dressed in motorbiker's gear, some of them only now pulling off their helmets. Des and Tony, who act as ushers on these occasions, are trying to find them seats, trying to encourage them to move forward to where there's an odd spare seat in a pew. But by the time the hymn is over, they have settled down together at the back, most of them standing, and a few sitting on the floor.

It's a Requiem Mass, and longer than most. Both priests are there and Father Crane leads the service sensitively, asking our special prayers for Moira and Paddy. We sing 'The Lord is my shepherd' and 'Abide with me', then after communion we hear a taped song. I listen to the words and realise I've heard this sweet and sentimental song many times on the radio. It tells me that for every drop of rain that falls, a flower grows, and seems to be suggesting that there must be a God because everything is so nice.

I've heard this song many times before, on the radio. It's sweet and sentimental and it seems to be more or less saying that there must be a God because everything is nice.

Knowing the tastes of my own children I feel pretty sure that this song would never have been a favourite of Damian's, and I guess it was Moira who wanted it played. I imagine she needs to believe that Damian had at least a faith in some sort of God. I look at her and although I am a long way behind her, I can tell she is crying. I start to cry myself.

Then there's a surprise. A young biker is walking down the aisle. He is wearing heavy boots, black jeans and a black leather jacket. He steps up onto the sanctuary and goes to the lectern where the microphone is. He faces the congregation and I see now that he has a bright open face. Then he looks across at Father Crane.

'Is it all right for me to say a few words, Vicar?' he asks. The 'Vicar' looks slightly apprehensive but he smiles and says, 'Yes, of course, go ahead.' Fr Joe is sitting in his place behind the young man and I see that he is grinning. There is absolute silence in the church as the biker begins:

'My name is Ed Taylor and Damian was my mate. I just want to tell you some things about him which you may not know. All of us bikers thought a lot of Damian, that's why we're here this morning. He was a good laugh and he was cool, but he was also a good friend. You could always count on Damian – he would never let you down.

Oh, I know he was no angel. He'd done his share of stupid things when he was younger, like most of us. And although he used to say, if it ever came up, that he was a Catholic, I know he didn't have much time for church. But Damian was a great guy and we all miss him. When we went away together, us bikers, to a camp somewhere, he used to play his guitar and sing. He had a great voice.

He thought the world of his mum and dad. We were all going off to France this summer, but

Damian said he couldn't come this time because he was saving up to buy something really nice for his mum on her birthday in October. He was like that.

We've brought a tape along and I'd like to play it now. It's a song Damian used to sing when we had little kids with us. I think it's called 'High Hopes'.' He signalled to someone at the back and the tape started.

I know this song well. Vincent used to sing it to the children years ago, when they were little. It's about a tiny ant who is determined to push over a great big rubber tree. Everyone knows this is impossible, but the ant has high hopes and suddenly, to everyone's astonishment, the huge tree falls over. Against all the odds, the little creature has succeeded. This happens because the ant has high hopes, so against all odds he succeeds. Everyone listened attentively to the words and when the song was over Ed was still standing there, smiling.

'I guess we all have high hopes for Damian,' he said. 'I don't know what you in this church believe, but me and my mates have high hopes that somehow we'll be together with Damian again one day.'

Mary Brown goes on Retreat

I think this is the most beautiful house I have ever seen. It was built in Elizabethan times, part brick, part stone, and although it has the remains of a moat and four little turrets, one at each corner of the roof, it isn't a great forbidding mansion. It looks friendly, homely even, and you can imagine a family living there, as they did, apparently, for centuries.

It was my friend Sally who persuaded me to come. She's been here lots of times; she says she prefers it to going on holiday. I didn't want to come, mainly because of Vincent. We've never been separated in all the long years of our marriage, except when I had to go into hospital once or twice, and it seemed unkind to leave him when he is feeling so low.

But Sally got the family on her side. They all agreed that I need a break, and Father Joe said it would be good for my soul, though he winked as he said it, so I think he was joking. But that's what retreats are for, isn't it? And there's no doubt that my soul could do with a bit of improvement or renewal or something … Anyway, Cathy said she would stay for the weekend and look after Vin, and it was only from Friday evening till Sunday afternoon, and I could always telephone to see if they were all right, so in the end I gave in and here I am in this wonderful place.

It's so peaceful. The house is miles from anywhere and surrounded by beautiful gardens. The air seems so fresh and clean, and I can't hear the noise of any traffic.

I'm just waiting for Sally. I have already registered and paid for the weekend. I feel guilty about spending so much on myself, but Vin, in one of his rare moments of humour, said it was worth it for a weekend's peace and quiet, for him!

I know I shouldn't feel shy, at my age, but I can't help it. The other people I've seen look so interesting and I guess they are not only much holier than me but also more intelligent. It will be an awful waste of money if I can't understand what the retreat-giver is saying. And suppose we have to answer questions?

But here comes Sally, looking happy and at ease.

'Isn't it wonderful to be here?' she says, and in spite of myself I catch something of her excitement and enthusiasm. We go inside and Sally leads the way through the fascinating house with its dark panelling and long corridors with portraits of the family on some of the walls and crucifixes and holy pictures on others. We climb up one set of stairs and I'm already out of breath before we tackle the next lot. My case is quite heavy because the weather can be so changeable at this time of year. I brought a thick sweater and a hot water bottle but the sun is shining and I was warm enough in a short-sleeved blouse in the garden just now.

Here we are at last. I put my luggage down and open the door of my room. I can't believe how small it is! It's certainly full of character, one in a row of little rooms tucked under the roof where the servants slept in days gone by. There's a sloping ceiling and a tiny diamond-paned window which is sadly too high for me to see out of. In one corner there's the smallest wash basin I've ever seen. The narrow single bed has a duvet with a pretty flowered cover and there's a beautiful icon of Mary and Jesus on the wall.

'Oh dear,' says Sally, 'I've never been up here before. I'm afraid my room is much nicer. It has marvellous views on two sides, and it's en suite. It's the one I usually have, on the first floor. She hesitates, and then says

'Look, Mary, why don't we swap? I'm sure all these stairs are bad for your knees, and you'd love my room. Besides, it would be good for me to have a change.'

It's kind of her, typical of her, but of course I

can't agree to that. I tell her I like my little room and that it will be fun up here. It's true. I do like the quaintness of it. And it feels good to have my own little space. But as soon as Sally's gone, I walk along the narrow corridor outside my room in search of a bathroom or a shower and a loo. There aren't any. Oh dear. That means I'll have to creep down those rickety stairs in the night.

We're going to have supper before the retreat starts properly. I have found the bathroom on the floor below and unpacked my things and opened the tiny window to let in the country air. I call for Sally in her splendid room. It's so grand – it was once called the master bedroom – that I wouldn't have felt at home in it anyway. We make our way downstairs and into a rather sombre room where people are settling down six to a table. I feel very shy now and keep close to Sally, hoping she'll sit by me. All the other people seem to know one another.

Sally leads the way to a table and introduces me to Ann and Robert. She is a teacher and he is a solicitor and they both seem pleasant and genuinely interested in me though I can't imagine why. There's also a plump little nun who introduces herself as Miranda, and a very pretty young girl with masses of frizzy blond hair and a low-cut crimson dress. I am very surprised to learn that none of them has been to Hazeldean Manor before, and only Miranda and Jane, the young girl, have been on a retreat before.

This cheers me considerably – I don't feel so awkward and shy any more but when the food comes my spirits wilt. I'm ashamed to say that one of the reasons I was persuaded to come to Hazeldean was the thought of not having to think about food, to buy it or to cook it, but my first taste of this soup makes me wish I was slaving over my own hot stove!

The soup is tepid, thin and watery, something between grey and brown in colour with little globules of grease floating on top. I hope for better things from the second course, but we are presented with lentil loaf and lettuce, unwashed it seems, from the vegetable garden. I never did like lentils but I'm hungry and I try not to think about what I'm eating and listen to the conversations around me.

The last course is fruit. In a bowl there are two small oranges, two wizened apples, and two glowing nectarines. I never buy nectarines, they're too expensive, but I've eaten them once or twice in other people's houses and they are delicious. Someone passes the bowl to Sally. She takes one of the nectarines. I see the bowl coming towards me. I think, 'I want that nectarine'. Then I think 'But wouldn't it be selfish to take it?' I'm just telling myself that if I don't take it, it will be because I don't want *others* to think I'm selfish – when a hand reaches out, takes the nectarine, and solves my problem. To my surprise it's the nun called Miranda. I end up with one of the mangy apples.

After supper we all gather in the Long Gallery. When I walk in there I am taken aback by the graciousness of this room. It has long windows all along the garden side and chandeliers hang from the exquisite plaster ceiling. There's a polished wood floor and a great fireplace with a glorious arrangement of different yellow flowers in the hearth. The room is warm but not hot, and extremely comfortable-looking chairs, covered in the same soft blue as the silky material of the curtains, are arranged in a circle. My spirits have ceased to wilt.

Bravely I choose a chair which is not next to Sally or any of my table companions, and wait eagerly for Fr Prentice to arrive. Fr Martin Prentice seems to be the reason why most, if not all the other retreatants are here. Apparently he is internationally known as an excellent retreat-giver. He is also, according to Sally, charming, friendly, prayerful, witty and always full of new ideas. I can't help feeling slightly sceptical – he sounds more like a superstar than a priest.

There's an expectant hush as the door opens punctually at eight o'clock. In comes, not Fr Martin, but the Warden of Hazeldean, a cheerful fellow who gave us a warm welcome when we arrived. He is followed by an old woman with a very lined face and spectacles and white hair. He looks embarrassed and says, 'I'm really sorry, everyone, to be the bearer of bad tidings. But I'm afraid we've had a message to say that poor Fr Martin has been suddenly called away to a funeral.

There is a deep-felt sigh from almost everyone present, a sigh I guess of some sympathy and huge disappointment.

'However,' continues the Warden, 'we are very fortunate indeed that our friend Ellen, Ellen Delaney, has very kindly agreed to step in at the last minute.' He turned to the woman 'Ellen, we are most grateful.'

Nobody groans again, but I guess they would like to. Instead they smile politely, and try to look grateful, as the Warden introduces us to Mrs Delaney.

After the Warden has gone Mrs Delaney joins our circle taking the chair left for Fr Martin. I feel sorry for her. I can imagine how awful it must be in her position. But she doesn't look discomfited. She looks serene, tranquil. She smiles warmly as her eyes move round the circle, then she tells us her name is Ellen and asks us to tell her our names and something about ourselves. I hate this, and I hate it even more as one after the other people tell us about their interesting lives. When it comes to me I feel my face go red and I clear my throat nervously before I say, apologetically.

'My name is Mary and I'm just a wife and mother.' I was looking down as I mumbled this, but I look up and meet Ellen's eyes. She smiles broadly and says *'Just* a wife and mother?' I smile back. I feel better now.

When we have gone round the circle – there are twenty of us altogether – Ellen picks up a large bag, made of some sort of sacking material, that she has brought with her.

'I live by the sea,' she says, 'which is a great blessing. And I've brought some pebbles with me. I'll bring the bag round and ask you each to take one, and then hold it in silence.'

My pebble is quite big. It's a pinkish colour, smooth and an almost perfect oval. I stare down at it in my palm and decide that I like it.

Ellen herself is holding a small green pebble. 'I'd like you to think of your pebble as baggage, as something heavy to carry, something you've brought here to Hazeldean this weekend. Each of us, whatever situations we're in, must have come with some burdens, some anxieties to do with love or death, with family or friends. And if we're to benefit from this retreat, if we're to be renewed and grow, then just for the space of this weekend, we need to leave these worries behind, to say No to them, to stop them, as far as we possibly can, from lessening the value of this retreat.

At first I resist this. I feel I am being treated like an infant, that the pebbles are a silly gimmick. But gradually as the silence lengthens I allow myself to do as Ellen suggests. I hold my pebble and look at it and think first about Vin and then one by one, about all the other sources of anxiety in my life. I make a decision to let go, just for these few hours.

Ellen speaks again. 'Remember,' she says, 'letting go like this in no way diminishes the love you feel for someone or the validity of your caring. Indeed it could be that you will leave here renewed in strength and the capacity to love because you have been able to let go for a while and to concentrate on God and on where you are in your life.'

I stay quiet a while longer and then I take my pebble and add it to the pile that is growing in a corner of the room.

When we're all settled again and still quiet, for everyone is paying attention, Ellen says, 'Now I'm going to give you a text, and I'd like you simply to stay where you are and reflect on it in silence for a few minutes. The text is this: 'Do not be afraid.''

She smiles, 'Yes, it's very short,' she says, 'but there's plenty to think about.'

I am very surprised. For the first time it feels right, really right, that I have come to Hazeldean. Because this text, surely it's meant for me? Nobody else here seems to be the least bit afraid, or lacking in confidence. But I am. I know I am. And I know I shouldn't be. I should trust in God, really trust him absolutely. Oh, I don't mean to save me from sorrow or pain, or those I love from sorrow or pain. But I can trust him, can't I, to be with me through it all? Yes, I must learn not to be afraid.

I open my eyes and see that Ellen is no longer sitting where she was. Feeling slightly guilty, like a disobedient schoolgirl, I stop concentrating on God, and turn my head. Ellen is at the far end of the room, where there is a large display board fixed to the wall and made of some material like cork so that you can stick drawing pins into it without doing any harm. She's got some big sheets of paper with writing on them and she's putting them up there. I wonder what we'll have to do next. I realise that I'm beginning to enjoy myself.

Ellen comes back to the group. She tells us there are seven passages of scripture pinned to the wall, each of them containing the words 'Do not be afraid', and she asks us to go and look at them and read them carefully and then choose one for our own study. She says when we have chosen our text we can find it in the bible (there are plenty of bibles in the Long Gallery and also in the Library) and then study it prayerfully. She would like us to bring it with us to the group tomorrow morning. She adds that she will stay while we choose our passages, so that if any of us needs help she'll be here.

I want to do this really well. I take a long time to choose my passage, and in the end it's between Isaiah 43, 'Do not be afraid, for I have redeemed you, I have called you by your name, you are mine', which I love, and Mark's description of Jesus walking on the water, where he called out, 'Courage, it is I! Do not be afraid.'

At last I make up my mind to choose the Mark but I know I need help so I go over to Ellen, who happens to be free, and I decide to be completely honest although I may look a fool. So I say, 'I'm afraid I don't know what it means, to study prayerfully.'

Ellen asks me to sit down next to her and she explains that it's a good idea to read the passage over and over, slowly digesting it and each time really thinking about the words. She says it may happen that some word or phrase in particular jumps out at me, and if it does, I can dwell on that and its meaning for me because this may be God's way of speaking to me through scripture.

On the other hand, Ellen says, I may like to use my imagination. In a panic, I wonder if I have any! But Ellen explains that I may be able to imagine myself in the scene, for example as one of the disciples in the boat.

I tell her I will try and she laughs and says, 'Don't try too hard!' When we are all back in the circle again, she says that we're probably all pretty tired, so we'll finish the evening with a quiet time of prayer.

She asks us to relax and she begins to play some peaceful music on a tape recorder. Then from somewhere she takes quite a big candle, lights it and asks the young girl, Jane, to turn out all the lights. We sit quietly for a moment or two and then Ellen says, 'We will pass the candle round the circle. As each person holds it, and please don't rush through this – we will all pray for that person. When you are holding the candle you may if you wish, say a short prayer aloud but there's no need to do this if you'd rather not.

At first I feel embarrassed. I have never done anything like this. But the whole atmosphere is so gentle and so accepting that I begin to feel calmer and when I am holding the candle, although it takes all my courage, I manage to say the word 'Vincent'. I am sad when the lights come on again and it is all over.

Ellen says, 'Tomorrow morning we'll start with a bit more lively liturgy. If anyone has brought any musical instruments or has any suggestions perhaps they'd like to stay behind. Oh, and by the way, there's coffee available in the room next to the library.'

I have no suggestions for the liturgy – I hardly know what liturgy is – and I don't think I want coffee, not if it's anything like the rest of the food here, so I think I'll just slip off to bed. But as I'm going out of the door Sally catches hold of my arm.

'Go up to my room, Mary,' she whispers 'I've got a surprise for you. I'll only be a few minutes.'

I don't really want to. Suddenly I'm longing for bed in my funny little room in the servants' attic. But Sally has been so kind, bringing me here …

I trudge up to her room and again I'm surprised at the luxury of it. There's a pale pink carpet with a discreet pattern, a wardrobe that's surely a real antique, and various standard lamps and two easy chairs. I have just sat down when there's a tap on the door and before I can say anything, to my astonishment a man comes into the room, carrying a bottle of wine.

'Hello! It's Mary, isn't it?' he says, smiling and holding out his hand. 'No, don't get up. I expect Sally's discussing the liturgy. She's quite brilliant, as I expect you know.' He realises that I'm peering at his name badge.

'Oh! Sorry!' he says. 'I'm Gerry, Gerry Hansom. I'm an old friend of Sally's. We've been meeting each other for years at Hazeldean. In fact I don't know what I'd do without the old place. It keeps you on the right track, and all that, don't you think?'

I'm a bit out of my depth. Of course I recognise Gerry now as one of our group, but I hadn't particularly noticed him when we all introduced ourselves. There are only a few men in the group, five I think, but now that he's face to face and close up, Gerry seems a most unlikely retreatant. He must be in late middle age but his hair shows no signs of grey. It is well brushed with a neat parting. He is wearing a tie and a blazer with brass buttons and I could see myself in the polish of his shoes if I wanted to.

I smile nervously and I'm relieved to hear Sally's

voice just outside the door, saying goodnight to someone. She comes in as full of energy as I'm drained of it.

We have a kind of feast together. I drink three glasses of wine and hungrily eat some delicious cheese and biscuits and olives that Gerry and Sally have brought between them. Gerry tells jokes and we seem to laugh a lot.

Then most surprising of all, Gerry suddenly turns serious. 'I'm having a problem with prayer, Sal,' he says.

Again I realise how tired I am. I quietly slip out of the room and to my shame find I'm a little bit woozy. I don't often drink wine at all, let alone three glasses. However, to my relief the lights of the stairs and corridors are all switched on and I manage to clamber unsteadily to my room. Then I glance at my watch. I see that it's after midnight. Without washing, without praying, I tumble into bed and fall instantly asleep.

When I walk into the dining room late next morning, I search in vain for Sally. I look for the others I met at table the night before, but I can see no spare seats. Then I hear a friendly voice.

'Mary! Over here!' It's Gerry, looking as immaculate as ever in a clean shirt with a different tie and matching silk handkerchief in his blazer pocket. He introduces me to the others at the table. Ann and Robert are there and they seem genuinely pleased to see me.

'Breakfast here's not as dire as supper,' says Gerry and he shows me where to get cereal and toast.

I don't see Sally until we're assembled in the Long Gallery again. She doesn't look as bright and bushytailed as Gerry, but she gives me a grin. She is sitting at the front in an ordinary chair with a clarinet in one hand.

I didn't know she could play any instrument, but when she begins I'm astonished at how beautifully the music flows. There are other instruments: two guitars and a violin. At first while people are still coming in, there is simply a joyous tune, but once we are all together with hymn sheets in hand we begin to sing 'Morning has broken' to some words that are new to me. I find myself singing with full voice.

Someone reads a poem they have written themselves about the courage of a child with leukaemia – Ann whispers to me that it is his own child who has died. Then we sing 'Do not be afraid' and next the young girl, Jane, sings a solo. It is in Irish, so I don't understand the words, but it is haunting.

We finish by singing 'Jubilate' and the 'band' accompanies us with all sorts of improvisations. As we sit down, a youngish man called Rory, who was at our table for breakfast, takes the chair next to me and he says, 'You have a lovely singing voice, Mary'. Normally I would have blushed and denied it, but for some reason I simply say, 'Thank you.'

Funnily enough, Ellen talks to us for a few moments about gifts. I could hardly believe it when she says, 'Of course we all know about certain obvious talents like Sally's musical flair and Mary's singing voice.' And she goes on to talk about unseen and unsung gifts, like smiling, listening, praying – even thinking about someone. Then she says, 'But let's get back to our main theme – fear and courage. I'd like you to take your chosen pieces of scripture and go somewhere – anywhere you like, inside or out, but on your own, to pray through your passage. Then at eleven o'clock, there's real coffee next to the library, and we'll all meet again at half past.'

I go into the garden. It's a beautiful morning and although I take a cardigan I doubt if I'll need it. I cross the lawn – it's still wet with dew – and make my way to a great tree with a smooth silvery bark and reddish leaves. I think it's a copper beech. There's a wooden bench under it and it's a good distance from the house so I decide to make it my place for study. It's hard at first. I'm not used to country sights and sounds and it all seems so wonderful that I just want to soak it all in and forget about my text.

But eventually I get down to it. I read the story very slowly, then read it again. The third time it happens just as Ellen said it might. Some words seem to leap from the page, just four words, 'their minds were closed'.

I think about this for a very long time, and realise how important it is to be open – to have not only an open mind but also an open heart to love and open hands to give. I ponder on all that this means in my own life. When I look at my watch I find it's already nearly half past eleven. I've missed coffee, but I don't mind. I hurry back to the group.

I realise I'm feeling happy. It was so peaceful in the garden and I feel at peace with myself. I believe I have learnt something worthwhile. But at Ellen's words this feeling evaporates quickly. She asks us to find a partner in the group, not someone we know well, and talk with them about our reflections.

For me, it would have been difficult enough to do this with Sally, and the thought of sharing my intimate thoughts with a stranger overwhelms me. People move around me, smiling, choosing their partners, but I sit where I am, gripped by a sort of panic, looking down. Then I feel a shadow over me and look up to see Miranda, the plump nun, grinning down at me and saying 'Should we go together, Mary?'

Negative thoughts about her rush into my head. 'She's fat, she's greedy, she took my nectarine, what a silly name for a nun', but of course I smile and stand up and we walk slowly outside together. Reluctantly I lead her to my special place under the tree.

It turns out that Miranda has been living in a shantytown in Ecuador until six months ago. She describes it to me – it sounds so terrible but I can tell that she loved it there. She got very ill and was near to death – 'I looked like a skeleton, believe it or not,' she says with a laugh. She was sent home when she came out of hospital and her Order allowed her to convalesce with her parents who live in Dublin. 'It was like being a child again,' she says, 'and they spoilt me rotten. They kept feeding me up, and although when I first came back I was horrified to see how much food and everything else is available over here, and how much choice there is compared with my people in Duran, I soon began to crave food and I ate and ate until – well, you can see, I'm gross. It's hard not to hate myself.'

Then she tells me how she chose the Isaiah passage,

and how she is afraid, very afraid to go back to her convent in Manchester where she will be bursar to the sisters and have to live the life she lived before Ecuador.

Somehow, there isn't any time left to talk about me, but I don't mind. I like Miranda now, I like her very much, but I don't feel a particular need to share my reflections with her.

Back in the Long Gallery, Ellen tells us that in the afternoon we will be free to do whatever we like until after tea – to rest or walk or pray or go into the town. She says she will be available in her room for anyone who would like to come and talk to her, and I decide I will be first in the queue for this. I would love to tell Ellen about my prayer time under the tree.

It doesn't work out that way. After lunch I volunteer to help with the washing up and so does Vernon, the man who wrote the poem about his daughter who died. He talks to me about her and about his fears and hopes and his wife and his work. The washing-up was finished long ago, but I feel I can't leave Vernon abruptly. I don't want him to feel hurt or rejected even by someone like me who means nothing to him. In the end he apologises for taking up my time and says I have been a great help. This seems silly, as I've said nothing, only listened.

I hurry upstairs to Ellen's room. To my dismay, three of our group are outside the door, waiting to see her. I hesitate, then decide to come back later. It seems all wrong to waste this beautiful afternoon sitting in a corridor, so I go outside again exploring the gardens. I come back after half an hour to find two different people waiting to see Ellen. I give up and go in search of the chapel.

At first I am disappointed. I had thought the chapel would be in keeping with the rest of the house, with beautiful old carvings in wood and stone, lovely stained glass perhaps. I expected it would be rather dark and mysterious.

So it is a shock to find a completely modern room, light and round, with white-washed walls and large windows through which I can see the sky and some trees. Everything in the room is simple and plain and a bowl of fresh flowers from the garden make the only splash of colour. I sit on a low stool and relax, quietly absorbing the tranquil atmosphere, doing nothing, resting in God, opening my mind and heart to him, listening. I don't know how long I stay there but when I hear a bell ringing in a distant part of the house I realise it must be tea time.

After a cup of tea and a biscuit – how can I be so hungry when I'm doing nothing? – we meet again in the Long Gallery.

Ellen tells us that we all look more relaxed than we did on Friday night but she goes on to say that she doesn't believe a retreat has been really helpful if it's just about feeling good. 'Of course it's wonderful if we can learn to accept ourselves as we are, if we can truly believe that our God loves us without condition, if we can trust without fear,' she says. 'But being a Christian is not just about being at peace with ourselves, indeed we can never be lastingly at peace as long as we only look inwards. We have to take up our cross, which means looking outward, means being concerned in the lives of those around us, means being involved in the suffering of our world. She reminds us that Jesus did a lot of his teaching by telling stories and she says it is amazing how much we can learn from one another. Then she invites anyone who is willing to tell us a story. She says it is only fair to start the ball rolling herself and she tells us about her son who is in prison. I am taken aback to hear this. Ellen is obviously such a good and wise person and it seems incredible that a child of hers would have committed a crime. Then she goes on to give us some startling and horrifying information about life under the prison system.

We are quiet for a moment when Ellen has finished speaking, then Ann tells us about her work in

Uganda among people with HIV and AIDS, and Miranda tells us about her shanty town in Ecuador, and a man called Wilfrid tells us how he had to give up the farm that had been in his family for generations because he was simply too poor to carry on. I think, I don't have any story to tell.

But in the quiet liturgy that follows, we are invited to pray aloud and I am not afraid. In front of all these others I pray for myself that I may become more aware of issues of justice and willing to take action when I can.

At the end Robert reads from Isaiah, where it says:

'If you give your bread to the hungry
and relief to the oppressed
your light will rise in the darkness
and your shadows become like noon.'

It is Sunday, time for lunch. But I excused myself from lunch. I wanted to savour the peace and beauty of this place for one more half-hour. I wanted to reflect on everything that's happened and to think how it will affect my life. I'm holding my pink pebble – they were given back to us at Mass. It's a sort of souvenir, I suppose, and I like it.

Yesterday evening was fun. We entertained one another, at least some of us did. I just watched and listened. Vernon played the piano, he's an excellent musician, and Wilfrid recited a funny monologue. Jane sang a solo, and then Ellen turned out to be a fantastic juggler. Gerry and Sally read a poem they had written together. There was wine to drink, again, but this time I only had one small glass. By eleven o'clock I felt extremely tired, but when I lay down on my narrow bed I found I couldn't sleep. After a while I put on my bedside lamp and for the first time looked properly at the icon facing me. I saw the infinite tenderness with which Mary held and gazed at her baby, and I knew it was with this same tenderness that God looked at me. I switched off the light and fell asleep.

Most of the morning was taken up with Mass. Of course if he had been here Fr Prentice would have been the celebrant, but in the event a young African priest turned up. His skin was very black and when he smiled, which he did nearly all the time, his teeth were dazzling. We spent a long time preparing. Father Mpinga gave us a little talk about the joyfulness of Mass in his own country and he showed us some dance steps for the entry procession which included a lot of us, even me, because very reluctantly, I had agreed to sing a duet with Jane.

It was an amazing Mass; I still feel a little bit

dizzy thinking about it. There was dancing, lots of singing, lots of flowers, a reading from scripture and one from T. S. Eliot which I didn't completely understand, a short smiling sermon, and at the Sign of Peace we all went mad, everyone hugging everyone. I liked it, I loved it, but at the same time I feel quite thankful that it isn't like that every Sunday.

Of course I am longing to get home to Vincent, and yet I am also really sad to be leaving Hazeldean. And it's only partly the beautiful house and garden and their peaceful, prayerful atmosphere. It's only partly the extraordinariness of it all. Mostly I'm sad to leave the people, the new friends I have made, friends who are on my wavelength, who take me as I am.

Ellen has already left. She said I could write to her. Miranda and Ann and Robert gave me their addresses and promised to keep in touch. I know I won't be able to afford to come again, but I'm hoping we can meet some other way.

I ask myself: what has this retreat done for me? I think it has brought me closer to God, deepened my trust in him and my confidence in myself. I hope it has really opened my mind and my heart and my hands. I have made one simple resolve: to join the justice and peace group in our parish.

Sally is coming across the grass with Gerry, dear

Gerry. He's sporting a bright yellow tie and matching handkerchief today. He gives me a big hug, holding me so tight I'm afraid my ribs will crack.

Sally and I walk slowly to her car. As we drive away I turn round and wave like a child, at no one in particular, at the house, perhaps, until we are round a bend and on the road. I turn to face the front and think how wonderful it will be to see Vincent again.